Break in Case of Silence

NEW WRITING SCOTLAND 39

Edited by
Rachelle Atalla
and
Marjorie Lotfi

Gaelic editor:
Maggie Rabatski

For Brian Hamill

Association for Scottish Literary Studies

Association for Scottish Literary Studies
Scottish Literature, 7 University Gardens
University of Glasgow, Glasgow G12 8QH
www.asls.org.uk

ASLS is a registered charity no. SC006535

First published 2021

British Library Cataloguing in Publication Data

A CIP record for this book is available
from the British Library

ISBN 978-1-906841-46-1

The Association for Scottish Literary Studies
acknowledges the support of Creative Scotland
towards the publication of this book

Typeset in Minion by ASLS
Printed by Bell & Bain Ltd, Glasgow

CONTENTS

INTRODUCTION

And just like that, another year rolls around and we are finalising the work to be included in *New Writing Scotland* 39. Except we're still living under the cloak of COVID-19 and pandemic conditions. The initial shellshock may have receded, and we have somewhat adjusted to our 'new normal', but we continue to navigate through uncertain terrain and loss. We are mourning both for our loved ones and for a way of life that has suddenly and unrecognisably been altered; this virus finding our own personal and collective Achilles' heel and allowing no one to escape its touch. However our resilience has grown, our perception and sense of community has intensified, and we're beginning to have much needed conversations about accessibility and inclusion thanks to the digital platforms we have become so accustomed to. Our approach to bringing this anthology together was to let the writing take the lead and curate a collection of work showcasing an array of emotions in an attempt to capture beautiful and often painful portrayals of life and human connection.

We received over seven hundred anonymous submissions this year and it was a delight and privilege to be allowed to read them. There is nothing quite like the feeling of stumbling across a piece of literary art that stops you in your tracks, demands your attention and lingers on in your mind long after its conclusion. This is the joy of editing *New Writing Scotland*, and certainly, as expected, this year's submissions did not disappoint. We were overwhelmed by the quality of work and inspired by the creativity born through shared and difficult circumstances. Oliver Emanuel's *Mountain Story* brings a disturbingly familiar sense of unease and confusion to a fictional community affected by immediate change. *Kindling* by Juliet Lovering and *Period Pain* by Niamh Griffin both beautifully and subtly explore loss, while Rob McInroy's *Fresh Watter* does an excellent job of addressing the silence that often surrounds our internal struggles. Tracey S. Rosenberg's *The Western Wall* considers identity and its relationship to place, something we're all perhaps contemplating, particularly in the light of Brexit and the renewed question surrounding Scotland's independence. But much like the reality of life there was laughter too, including Joshua Lander's *This is the Most Beautiful Love Letter Ever Written*, reminding us of our need for humour even in our darkest moments.

The poems included also reflect these strange and uneasy times. Patrick Errington's *Calling a Wolf a Wolf* and Lorcán Black's *Lockdown* hold the tension of being bottled up, while watching the world 'burning/but flying over'. Antonia Kearton's *A Benediction* reminds us how, in these times of stillness, the objects at hand can help us bring back the past, while Lauren Pope's *The Times I Didn't Use My Name* points out that sometimes we just want to shed memory and let it go. Poems like Michele Waering's *gauze street havers* bring us straight into looking hard at a place, noticing what is still right beneath our feet, and Christie Williamson's *return* feels a fitting tribute to now, how this world often feels like we're trying to play tennis without a net, that the trick is to remember that 'whatever falls/rises again'.

The same week we write this introduction there is news of the UK government's intention to cut funding to education in the arts, highlighting this notion held by some that the arts is unessential, disposable, to be considered as merely a hobby. But where would we be through the lockdowns, isolations and bereavements if it were not for the comfort and power of the arts? The need for words, poetry and storytelling has never been stronger. Perhaps it is our best asset in fighting inequality, exclusion and hatred, because by immersing ourselves in other people's worlds we can begin to understand their struggles and perspectives.

We hope you enjoy reading *New Writing Scotland* 39.

Rachelle & Marjorie

NEW WRITING SCOTLAND 40:
SUBMISSION INSTRUCTIONS

The fortieth volume of *New Writing Scotland* will be published in summer 2022. Submissions are invited from writers resident in Scotland or Scots by birth, upbringing or inclination. All forms of writing are welcome: autobiography and memoirs; creative responses to events and experiences; drama; graphic artwork (monochrome only); poetry; political and cultural commentary and satire; short fiction; travel writing or any other creative prose may be submitted, but not full-length plays or novels, though self-contained extracts are acceptable. The work must not be previously published or accepted for publication elsewhere, and may be in any of the languages of Scotland.

Submissions should be uploaded, for free, via Submittable:

nws.submittable.com/submit

Prose pieces should be double-spaced and carry an approximate word-count. Please do not put your name on your submission; instead, please provide your name and contact details, including email and postal addresses, on a covering letter. If you are sending more than one piece, please group everything into one document. **Please send no more than four poems, or one prose work.**

Authors retain all rights to their work(s), and are free to submit and/or publish the same work(s) elsewhere after they appear in *New Writing Scotland*. Successful contributors will be paid at a rate of £20 per published page.

Please be aware that we have limited space in each edition, and therefore shorter pieces are more suitable – although longer items of exceptional quality may still be included. Our maximum suggested word-count is 3,500 words.

Seonaidh Adams
SAORSA BHO DHAORSA?
30 Bliadhna bho Aonadh na Gearmailt

Tha mise shuas gu leòr nam bhliadhnaichean 's gu bheil cuimhn' agam air a' Chogadh Fhuar. Thuig mi na dh'fhaodadh tachairt nan tigeadh cuisean gu h-aon 's gu dhà. Chunnaic mi an dràma *Threads* a nochd dhuinn an fhìrinn lom mu na thachradh dhuinn is buille niùclasach san dùthaich againn. Bha mi nam dheugaire sna h-80an. Bha mi air ceòl punc a lorg. Chuala mi na sgeulachdan air a' bhus agam do na geamaichean Hearts bho na meinnearan a bha air stailc. Dubh-ghràin air Thatcher agus strì ris a' phoilis. Bha aimhreit air sràidean Shasainn. Bha heroin pàilt sna bailtean mòra agus bha an tinneas 'ùr' a bha seo – AIDS – mu sgaoil. Bha na milleanan gun chosnadh. Amannan dubha.

Bha na bh'agam de dh'eòlas air Bloc an Ear na Roinn Eòrpa bho na meadhanan an-seo. An-dràsta 's a-rithist, gheibhinnsa litir no clàr-fada punc bho chuideigin sa Phòlainn no Iùgoslaibhia. Bha an aon duan ri chluinntinn ge-tà: 'tha na Comannaich a cheart cho dona ri na Nàsaich'. Bho na chunnaic mise, bha iad ceart.

Deichead gu leth as dèidh sin, choinnich mi ri mo chèile a bhuineas do Shacsanaigh san t-seana DDR – no Poblachd Dheamocratach na Gearmailt. B'e mo chiad cheist 'Ciamar a bha d'àrach?'

'Glè mhath', fhreagair i, 'bha mi gu math sona sna seann làithean'.

Ged a bha mi a-riamh mothachail air an olc a thàinig an lùib a' chalpachais againne, cha do bhuail e nam inntinn a-riamh gun robh sonas idir air a bhith anns na dùthchannan an Ear a bha siud. Bha siud ann gun teagamh sam bith agus feumar a ràdh gu bheil tomhais mhath de shearbhachd ann san là an-diugh am measg an t-slòigh aig a bheil eòlas air an dà shiostaim.

Tha am baile às a bheil mo chèile na shuidhe mu uair a thìde de shiubhail an ear air baile mhòr Dhresden. Mus d'thàinig 'saorsa' bha mu 40,000 neach a' còmhnaidh ann – tòrr dhiubh ag obair san iomadh factaraidh a bha ann. Tha san là an-diugh mu 25,000 air fhàgail. Tha na factaraidhean bàn agus a' dol nan tobhtaichean. Mar an ceudna, tha agus mòran den taigheadas ann. Chaidh teanamantan agus blocaichean thaigheadais fhàgail falamh. Àiteachan math airson pàrtaidhean sna 90an mas e deugaire a bh'annad aig an àm sin ach a-nis tha tòrr dhiubh a' tuiteam am broinn a-chèile. Thog an luchd-còmhnaidh orra a Bherlin, a Dhresden no dhan àird an Iar a shireadh saorsa is soirbheachas no mar bu choltaiche dìreach teachd-a-steach.

Bidh mise, mo chèile agus ar clann a' tadhal air baile a h-àraich dhà no trì tursan gach bliadhna. Tha mi a' sìor ionnsachadh mun àite, na cleachdaidhean agus an eachdraidh.

Tha màthair mo chèile na tidsear agus bha sna seann làithean. Air sgàth sin, gheibh i tuarastal nas ìsle na iadsan aig nach eil ceangail ri teagaisg san DDR. A thaobh 'saorsa', tha i eadar dà bheachd. Bha a-riamh miann aice a bhith a' siubhail dhan Fhràing – cha b'urrainn dhi siubhal ach dhan ear ro-làimhe – agus gu follaiseach tha sin a' còrdadh rithe. Ach, bha an obair aice na b'fheàrr sna seann làithean agus cha robh iomagain aice mu theachd-a-steach. Tha i an impis an obair aice a leigeil dhith agus gheibh i peinnsean. Ach a-rithist, bha na peinnseanan na b'fheàrr sa DDR.

A thaobh athair mo chèile, thilleadh esan air ais do làithean an DDR nam b'urrainn dha. Dh'obraich esan san fhactaraidh aig Robur a rinn làraidhean is carabadan troma mar sin. Aig toiseach nan 80an, fhuair a theaghlach flat ann an aon de na blocaichean ùra a thogadh. Mar na teaghlaichean eile, bha iad air an dòigh. A bharrachd air sin, chluich e ann an sgioba ball-coise an fhactaraidh san dàrna lìg aig an DDR. Aon seusan, is e 'cluicheadair na bliadhna', fhuair e turas a Leningrad mar dhuais. Bha a h-uile càil a dh'fheumadh e aige san DDR – obair sheasmhach, taigh, airgead, ball-coise agus saor-làithean air a' Bhaltic no shìos an Iùgoslaibhia.

Tha bratach an DDR agus seann bhratach an USSR fhathast shuas sa gharaids aige.

Tha bana-charaid aig an teaghlach air an aon ràmh. Sna 80an, chaidh ise na togalaiche agus an uairsin na h-ailtire. Tha i fhathast ag obair aig a' chomhairle ann am planadh taigheadais. Ach, sa DDR cha robh e na annas airson boireannach a bhith sa cheàrd-to-gail no bhith an sàs ann an obair 'throm' eile mar obrachadh chrann-thogail. Cia mheud boireannach a chunnacas am Breatann nan 80an ri obair mar sin? Ged a tha i sàsaichte le beatha an-dràsta, tha i diombach nach d'thàinig an saoghal-bràth de chothroman is de bheartas a gheall Helmut Kohl, ceannard na Gearmailt an Iar, nuair a thadhail e air an DDR mus d'thàinig aonadh. 'A bheil sibh ag iarraidh aonadh na Gearmailt? A bheil sibh ag iarraidh soirbheachais?' thuirt e.

Thog an triùir a tha sin an Treuhand mar chùis-ghearain. Se sin an *quango* a bha an urra ris an dà eaconomaidh a thoirt ri chèile. Ach, se a thachair 's gun deach sealbh agus talamh nan daoine – oir sann aig poblachd an DDR a bha am fearann, na companaidhean agus na co-chomainn – a reic ri companaidhean mòra an Iar air prìsean suarach. Chì iadsan e mar *asset-stripping*.

An-uiridh nuair a chunnaic sinn cuid sa Ghearmailt a' dèanamh gàirdeachais is iad a' comharrachadh an là a thuit 'Balla Bherlin', dh'fhaighnich mi dhem chèile 'Eil na pàrantan agad a-muigh no aig pàrtaidh?'

'Chan eil gu dearbh,' fhreagair i, 'se àm dorcha a bha sin. Cha robh obair aca ged a bha teaghlach aca ri bhiadhachadh. Cha do dh'fhàg iad an dùthaich ach dh'fhàg an dùthaich iadsan.'

A rèir cunntas-bheachd a rinneadh 10 bliadhnaichean air ais am measg dhaoine a dh'fhuirich san DDR, thuirt 57% gum b'fheàrr leotha sòisealachd.

Tha pàrantan is caraidean mo chèile air an ràmh seo gun teagamh sam bith. Chan e 's gun robh a h-uile càil foirfe ach bha aca na dh'fheumadh iad. A-nis, tha leth-bhràth aca – tuarastalan agus peinnseanan nas ìsle na Gearmailtich bhon iar – agus seirbhisean poblach a tha suarach an taca ris na bh'ann san DDR. An àiteachan, tha an òigridh air gabhail ri poileataigs an làimh-dheis mar fhreagairt air seo.

Chan fhacas tilleadh phoilitigeach fhathast ged a tha aon phàrtaidh – *die Linke* – aig a bheil ceangail ri pàrtaidh riaghaltais an DDR a' co-riaghladh ann an aon stàit. Tha àireamhan nan daoine aig a bheil cuimhne air na feartan 'math' den DDR a' sìor fhàs nas lugha agus chan eil gluasad mòr gu leòr gus an siostam sin a thoirt air ais ged a tha mirean dheth ri lorg.

Bha cùram-cloinne air leth cudromach san DDR agus mar a h-uile càil, cha mhòr, bhon t-seana shiostaim, chaidh cur às dha nuair a chaidh an dà Ghearmailt aonadh. Nuair a mhol cuideigin sa phàrlamaid ùr aonaichte sna 90an gum biodh cùram-cloinne na bhuannachd do theaglaichean òga, chaidh a chàineadh mar 'Chomannach'. A-nis, tha e air ais agus tha fèill mhòr air.

Bha an sgrìobhadair cliùiteach Günter Grass an aghaidh aonadh na Gearmailt. Bha esan air uabhasachadh air mar a bha companaidhean mòra bhon taobh siar deiseil gus na co-chomainn a cheannachd air prìs ìosal, uidheaman a thoirt às agus an luchd-obrach a thilgeil air an dùnan. Thuirt e gur e 'bargan' a bh'ann agus nach b'e aonadh a bh'ann ach '*annexation*'.

An sùil mo chuimhne-sa, b'e na h-80an àm dorcha ged a chaidh mo thogail san Iar ann an calpachas is 'saorsa'. Do theaghlach mo chèile ge-ta, se na 90an a bha dubh is dorainneach. Ged a tha na mòr-bhùthan aca a-nis làn de gach seòrsa bìdhe is faoineasan air nach eil feum, tha mòran ann fhathast den bheachd gun robh na làithean geala aca còrr is 30 bliadhna air ais. Saoilidh mise gum b'urrainn do dh'Alba is dùthchannan beaga eile rudeigin ionnsachadh bhon DDR.

Lorcán Black
THE DISAPPEARING WOMAN

'*Nothing*', they say: '*No trace.*'
And for weeks we turn over the park,

the nearby farms, the fields.
Everywhere close to anywhere.

But eventually there are plates to wash,
kids to dress and each morning

school ties go up and under,
roundabout but even still,

we searched and searched silos, barns,
cornfields – we bent their full, dull, gold heads –

and far fields, car-trunks,
sheds – anything we could and for a while

it felt like every blade of grass knew a thing we didn't
and we couldn't sleep or move

without keeping an eye out
and eventually the river just kept on being a river

and in winter it looked dark
and kind of silver but no-one ever asked.

And still there are far fields,
the whitened silence of grass-blades each winter

and here a river, and how it kept on
being a river year after year –

though no-one ever fucking asked it
but it just does it anyway like some utter

fucking asshole who totally forgot
what it was we were even looking for to begin with.

And it kind of feels like someone
ought to throw him the fuck out of here

but the river goes on being a river –
year after year and each winter

the spring falls like a drunk,
giving us nothing, over and over.

And the river just slides over itself,
all silver and slick, as if it knows nothing.

And all of us stand here, pissed off,
swearing and staring at that damn river,

wishing maybe, if it all flowed the *right* way,
it could wash all this bullshit the flying fuck away.

LOCKDOWN

Look
how quiet it is here –
how tight the night bites you.

These small mouths –
how teeth their sharp, small

movements at dawn/sleepless
flour-fingers rolling white dough
& milk churning over & over –

pouring honey in coffee – (shop had no sugar) –
how we care to make a thing beautiful
enough to bear.

How for days & days
there is a new cupcake/a cake/
something with folds/with a softness –

anything sweet folded in on itself
like a baby, like a sweetness of faces/
families over a fence.

Spring months march heavy –
summer/winter
& weight, like long-still water,
like glass clouded over

& every morning
in the morning paper:
death in the news.

Dawn birds crying/
strange choir:

like a host of swallows
        burning
        but flying over.

Sheila Black
CLIMATE (7) (PAST TENSE)

dear small daughter for a long time I did not write
what had already become past-tense was past-tense
and I am sorry I was not able to hold it as one might
in a dream hold a stream of water and sing it to sleep
and I am sorry that I told you this image as if it were
in truth perdurable plangent and constant moon
over our seas when it is the shifting that matters.
dear small the birds the mockingbirds they sang
in the middle of the night and for this we cursed
them but then we came upon their nests in the black
of day noon when the sun is a diamond burning
through however much blue and the two of them
circled so tirelessly with their wings fanning the
turquoise eggs inside the nest of dead grass and we
understood we were not the only ones but even this
could not stop us from doing as we had done all
our lives long and the cars we pulled out of driveways
and the highways that took us into the buzzing
electric of buildings poured in dense concrete
and the cooling chemicals seeping and cycling
as though through calm artificial hearts and outside
unnoticed the ghost-blue of juniper needle and berry
and the ghost-rising of smoke from the fires we
claimed we had not set. dear daughter now that we
must use the past-tense for what we thought was ours
now as we move into the possible distance I open
my hand to give you this picture of two wings.

CLIMATE (10)

Down by the headgates, the crawfish cling
as the water sinks.

You might picture the sky here as a great cat,
golden lion eagerly lapping,

lapping. We are walking along the cracks in what
was once river bed,

by the headgates so many half-formed bodies.

The light here rises, mornings, as if we ourselves
were the source of all radiance.

I have no other way to say this – why I have loved you
so intensely. I believe in what preserves

itself any way it can. Those toads at the base
of my garden who buried themselves seven years

in the dry-as-dry of dust and when the floods came,
they rose up; yes, they rose

green-skinned and singing.

Kate Coffey
THE SÌTH

There were some lassies singing at the feeing fair. It was a bawdy song, and one of them – the bonniest of them – mimed and pulled her face. We all laughed. One of the lads dared me to offer her a kiss for a situation, for we knew of one or two going. We'd had a fair few drams by then; it always puts the devil in me.

She responded with a slap; she was a strong lass and my ears rang. She said she would obtain a situation on her own thank you kindly, and stamped the mud off her boots. The fiddle started up after that.

Thereafter a farmer came by and looked her up and down. You're a stout-looking hizzie, he said, what wage are you wanting? Five pounds, said she. When he laughed she jutted her chin. I'll give you four, my farmer called out to her from afar. If you pass interview with my wife, that is. Our house servant just took her leave.

The fiddle changed then, something mournful. But I was content for my fee had been met that day and the arles was in my pocket.

She sat there, shyly, lowering her eyes each time she answered a question.

Your current situation?

It has finished, madam.

The reason?

The master became ill.

The length of your service there?

She blushed and after a while I realised the mite couldn't count. Eventually she said, from this last Whitsunday.

I nodded. Are you familiar with scripture, Mary? I reached for it on the side and fixed my glasses to my nose.

Another blush.

I began to read aloud. *For she had said unto the servant, What man is this that walketh in the field to meet us? And the servant had said, It is my master: therefore she took a vail, and covered herself.*

She blinked at me and lowered her gaze again; I sighed and closed the book. The lass was evidently a dullard. But better that than one full of guile, for we'd had our fair share with the last.

You will attend church with us on the Sabbath, I told her.

She nodded.

She was sat at the back, two rows in front, next to Cook. I recognised her at once, and every week thereafter. The farmer and his wife always sat in front. When she turned I winked but she did not respond and walked the length home beside the farmer's wife.

On the harvest we needed all hands, so the farmer's wife released her from the house. We worked well into the night and the farmer was taking a dram, he sat on the bale and called on her to sing. He told her not to look so modest, for he had seen her performance at the feeing fair.

He glanced at me expectantly, so I called on her to sing too. She looked at me, then, and I think if she could have slapped me again, she would have. She jutted her chin, and began to sing a hymn but the farmer waved it away. For pity's sake, we're not dead yet, he said.

So she sang something else, something very melancholy, and the farmer's eyes misted over. She did have a bonny voice.

She was kneeling by the fireplace, her head lolling. I said her name sharply and she woke with a start, her eyes dark with shadows underneath. I asked her if she was ailing for something and she said no.

Cook had already woken me, complaining that Mary had not brought her the water-ewer this morning, which had set her late for breakfast. I did not make comment, for the servants can quarrel between themselves. Cook added that she had found elderflowers hidden in the kitchen, and what did I make of that?

I was dreaming; a nice dream with a young lass smiling to me and calling my name over and over. Then she put my hand to her breast and I felt I would die happily then and there.

Duncan, she said, and shook me awake. I reached for her, still in my dream, and she gave me a clout across the ear. She was out of breath and shivering. I will sleep up here this eve, she said.

What's the matter?

Nothing for you to concern yourself with, she said, and began pulling the straw around her.

I could not sleep after that, my ear was still throbbing, so I sat there, listening to the horse snuffle underneath us.

At church that Sabbath I could see a strand of straw poking out from under her hat, and it was all I could do not to reach over and extract it. I yawned and the minister pointed at me and instructed me to put on the whole armour of God to stand against the wiles of the devil.

I took her aside to speak to her about the laundry. I had my suspicion that Mary had embellished her previous situation, for the clothes were sopping and smelt dreadfully. Was the girl even acquainted with a mangle?

She put down the peat basket, her eyes fixed on the floor. I asked her to look at me then, for she was drawing my patience. When she did, a shiver went through me for I saw she had different coloured eyes, like the sìth. How had I not noticed previously? From then on I was guarded in my dealings with the girl.

She had one eye blue, the other green, I had never seen the like. They fixed me with their unearthly power and when she began to sing I clamped my hand to her mouth for fear the wind would be her accomplice and carry her voice down to the house.

Sing, he instructed, and I did, even though my cheek throbbed from his last strike.

I was waiting at the dyke for the farmer to approve the work but he did not arrive. So I sat awhile, to smoke my pipe, listening to the burn trickle down. I saw Mary down the bottom there. She was rinsing her face in the water and did not see me watching. Then she turned to face me and I waved but she did not wave back.

My husband does not look at me when he comes indoors, and sits in front of the fire. I follow him in and stand there. After a while he asks me to read from Peter.

They promise them freedom, while they themselves are slaves of depravity, I recite, my throat tightening.

He begins to sob then and puts his hands over his face. I slam the book shut and strike him with it again and again. Even though it is heavy I do not tire.

If they have escaped the corruption of the world by knowing our Lord and Saviour Jesus Christ and are again entangled in it and are overcome, they are worse off at the end than they were at the beginning.

I know the verse by heart, I need not read it.

Of them the proverbs are true: 'a dog returns to its vomit' and 'a sow that is washed returns to her wallowing in the mud'.

I have seen her stamping the mud from her boots, pulling up her skirts to do so.

(She is no better than the last one, Cook told me, worse if anything. She tosses and turns in the night, waking us up, and then sleeps past daybreak like the lady of the manor.)

I have seen her simpering as she pulls up her skirts to stamp her boots. It's bewitching is what it is. It would turn any Christian man into an animal. Into a dog.

For people are slaves to whatever has mastered them.

I was not in a dream this time she came up the ladder, though it felt so, as she smiled rather than scowled as was her custom, and sat by me. She even took a dram and we sat peaceably together drinking. I remarked about her hair, how it fell pleasantly about her neck just so, but she sat there staring into space like she was in some dream herself. So I began to sing:

> Bidh mo ghaol do Mhàiri Bhàn
> Dìleas, dùrachail gu bràth,
> Seinnidh sinn d'a cheil' ar gràdh;
> 'S tha mi 'dol 'ga pòsadh.[1]

She laughed then and I saw the swelling on her face. She took out some elderflower petals from her pocket and a slice of butter and began to rub them between her fingers until a paste formed, and she applied it to her cheek.

She called on me to sing again, so I sang a song about a poor lad who saved all his coins for a ship to Canada because his heart was broken by his highland lass. I then confessed more than I should have about my circumstances, hoping to impress her, as my tongue was loose with the whisky.

She listened to me, staring into space once again.

She was not at church the following Sabbath, nor the one after that.

One eve Cook brought out some mutton broth to the barn, which was unusual, normally she leaves it on the kitchen table, and

---

1   'Màiri Bhàn', John Roderick Bannerman

she stood there, hopping from one foot to the other. Unable to contain herself any longer she said, your bonny bird has flown, now how's about that. Seeing my face she then pinched my cheek and offered me some buttered bread.

INVERNESS-SHIRE KIRK SESSION MINUTES

OF NOVEMBER 29TH 1895

The Moderator stated that he had called this meeting because it was generally known that Mary Mackay, sometime domestic servant at Blair Farm near Inverness, was dismissed without fee from her position following allegations of impropriety, namely fornication. On being admonished to speak the truth, she declared that James Blair, Master at Blair Farm was the partner of her guilt, and furthermore that he was the father of the illegitimate child. The Moderator considered it right that some inquiry should be made into the particulars of so disgraceful a proceeding and the session highly approved of this being done and after some conversation directed their officer to summon James Blair before them on December 5th current at one o'clock.

I recounted, before the Session, the lengths to which we go in order to preserve the spiritual welfare of our servants. We keep them well versed in the Shorter Catechism, I said, and bring them to church and instruct them to keep the Sabbath in the proper manner. Both my wife and I go to great pains to discourage the servants from opportunities for loose conversation and other temptations to sin. But, I said, there are some wiles that even a shackle and chain can not contain, nor fear of God.

When pressed by the gentlemen, I made reference to Mary visiting the young lad in the barn after sundown. Witnesses can be produced, I added. Furthermore, in withholding her fee, the lass may have felt spite toward myself and my wife, and sought her revenge. Which is a sorry thing indeed, I said, considering our paternalistic endeavours.

The gentlemen nodded.

*

Sing, he instructed, and I did, even though my jaw throbbed from his last strike.

Sing, he instructed, and I did, even though the stench of whisky and mutton was on his breath.

His wife is known to bear testimony corroborative of the statement. Thus, disowning the paternity of the child the Moderator finds to be proper in this case and hereby absolves James Blair of the scandal. Taking into account the condition of Mary Mackay the Moderator recommends for her to partake one day and one night only on the stool of repentance, thereby advertising the consequences of wickedness and immorality to the local congregation.

The lass had a terrible voice as she stood there outside the Inn, swaying about and singing. One of the lads bent down to retrieve her as her knees buckled, but she held her mug aloft, singing louder.

The fair was in its dying embers now, but we were still in hearty spirit, for our fees had been met, or near enough and I had a position up in Abriachan. That is when I saw Mary, as we were gathered there outside the Inn, waving at me. I did not at first recognise her, as she was carrying a bairn, and when I went up to her I patted its head.

When was it born? I asked, surprised.

This February, she told me.

He needs a name, she added, and it may as well be yours.

I did not understand and told her so.

He needs a name, she said again, stamping her boot.

But I am not the bairn's kin, I said. My head was spinning by this point, less for the drink and more for this bewildering exchange.

I sat us both down and rubbed my forehead.

The bairn mewed and she shifted it about on her shoulder. She asked me plaintively for help, that she could pursue a paternity decree in the Sheriff Court for a new certificate of birth.

I repeated that I would help her if I could, but I had no wish to be named in Court and decreed for money I did not possess (this was not strictly true but I was damned if I was giving a solitary coin to this bewitching lass).

She said this was not her wish. If the court decrees aliment from you, she said, you have my solemn oath by God that I will not pursue it. *My solemn oath by God.*

She took my hand then and put it against her cheek. It was wet and I felt a great sadness then, for all that might have been.

It is your name I want, she assured me. Nothing else.

The new servant came on recommendation, which my husband felt was more in keeping with the purity and gravity of Christian discipleship, than the rowdy lassies hawking themselves at the fair. Tell me, I said to her, as she sat down, her eyes wide as saucers, are you familiar with scripture?

Oh, yes, madam, she said. I can recite some by heart.

I listened to the words of Ephesians eject from her mouth with its stubs of tooth. When she stopped she wiped her nose with a handkerchief. God forgive me but she was an ugly wretch and my heart took comfort in this.

Though my father's name was on my certificate of birth, because they were unmarried I have my mother's name. I do not remember her, yet by virtue of this she has imprinted herself upon me and upon all who come from me. It was my foster mother who told me she had died. She was coughing in a bed, she said, when she took me from her with a handkerchief over her nose and mouth.

She had one eye blue, and one eye green, like the sìth, she added.

My foster mother told me about their translucent wings and their cèilidhs amongst the heather. How at night you can hear music come out of the sìtheans where they dwell and singing too, she said. But they are shy folk and if you surprise them, you will beware, for they make a merry dance of mischief.

She didn't say any more, for she was a superstitious woman.

And grey-haired women tall and strong,
Erect and full of grace,
Meet mothers of a noble clan,
A brave and stalwart race,
And many a maiden young and fair,
With pallid, tear-stained face.

I do not hold a solemn oath by God, for I am not sure what God has done by us. What did He do when our clans were wrenched from the soil that they had worked for generations, soil that had their blood and toil and bones in it?

What did He do when these men starved of their ancestral land became wandering, ravenous animals and their sons after them?

No, I hold no solemn oath by God. I am more inclined to make a solemn oath by a rowan tree, or burn, or sìthean.

They met upon the river's brink,
By the church so old and grey,
They could not sit within its walls
Upon this sunny day;
The Heavens above would be their dome,
And hear what they would say.[2]

*

SHERIFF COURT FILIATION & ALIMENT DECREE, 16TH JULY 1896

At Inverness, the sixteenth day of July, eighteen hundred and ninety-six, in an action in the Sheriff Court of the Sheriffdom of Inverness, Elgin and Nairn at Inverness at the instance of Mary Mackay, sometime

---

2   'The Last Sabbath in Strathnaver before the Burnings', Annie Mackay

domestic servant at Farm of Blair, near Inverness, now residing at Dunrobin Street, Tain, against Duncan Chisholm, Crofter or labourer Caiplich by Abriachan in the parish and county of Inverness, Defender, the sheriff decreed the defender to pay to the pursuer the sum after-mentioned in respect he was the father of an illegitimate male child of which the pursuer was delivered at eighty church street Inverness on the tenth day of February eighteen hundred and ninety-six.

Two pounds ten shilling sterling with the legal interest thereon from the tenth day of February eighteen hundred and ninety-six two pounds ten shillings sterling with the legal interest thereon from the tenth day of February eighteen hundred and ninety-six for inlying charges and eight pounds sterling per annum for twelve years as aliment for said child payable said aliment quarterly in advance as from said date with interest on each instalment of the date of its becoming due till payment under deduction till payment under deduction of the sum of three pounds seven shillings sterling paid to account on said sums and four pounds sixteen shillings and seven pence sterling of expenses and the sheriff grants warrant for all lawful execution hereon by instant acquirement and also after by paying a charge of seven free days extracted at Inverness this thirty-first day of July eighteen hundred and ninety-six.

Sometimes I dream about my mother's translucent wings and when I wake I can still hear a fragment of the song she sings, drifting away.

Oliver Emanuel
MOUNTAIN STORY

You are the first person to notice the disappearance of the mountain.

Not yet six A.M. There's a mist. The sun is here, somewhere, but it's taking its time. Everything has a soft edge.

You're tired and empty, a little lightheaded. You know it would be better to eat before you leave the house but that would mean getting up closer to four which feels like too great a commitment to the thirty pounds a week you earn for handling the village's only paper round. Colin sometimes gives you one of the fresh morning rolls, but not today. You've had nothing since last night, not even a sip of water, so when you stop your bike on the white lines of the main road, look up to the great wide emptiness, you have to blink a few times to make sure you're not asleep or imagining things.

But no.

Definitely no mountain where previously there has been a mountain.

The luminous yellow bag, half-full of newspapers smelling of vinegary chips, hangs heavy at your side. There's a slight ache in your left shoulder. You only have two streets to go before you make the turn for home, get ready for school.

You feel ill-equipped to handle the situation, wishing there was an adult close by. You look up and down the road, hoping to catch an early-morning dog-walker.

No-one else is about.

Your mouth is incredibly dry.

You try to recall the last time you looked at it, properly looked at it. The thing about living in a village in the shadow of a mountain, you admit to yourself, is that you take it for granted that it will always be there. A mountain stays put. Or that's what you've always been told. But is that true? You frown. Has anyone ever explained the geology of mountains to you? People in the village talk about the mountain, of course. The village is nothing special in itself: a hundred households, a community centre, a newsagent's, a derelict tin church, and a bad pub with a ferocious dog called Angus. The village's main virtue is that it has a large car park to enable hikers, climbers and tourists access to the mountain. But now you consider it, you can't remember anyone telling you about the mountain. Its nature, its reality.

The mountain is a regular mountain as far as you're concerned.

Until it isn't.

*

Your mum had vertigo when she was pregnant with your little brother. She couldn't even get to her bed without feeling dizzy, having to lie down on the carpet in the living room or the kitchen floor, breathing through her nose, fingers gripping tightly to the ground. At the time, you'd found it funny, seeing her like that, you were only three years old, and had never seen your parent vulnerable. You'd thought she was playing a game. Now you feel it. That spinning sensation, a feeling of heaviness, of gravitational pull, a sick taste at the back of your throat.

You'd like to lie down on the wet tarmac, close your eyes.

You manage to finish your round – pushing the bike, stopping to take deep breaths – dropping the final papers to No. 4, No. 7, and one each to Mr and Mrs Ramsay at No. 28.

You glance left as you park your bike round the side of the house, expecting the mountain to reveal itself as the sun rises fully and the mist clears.

Still nothing.

No mountain.

*

What does it look like? Now it's gone, the mountain is curiously hard to picture in your mind. You must concentrate, fill in the impossible corona from memory. It's big. With a curved, almost beak-like summit. You once heard your dad compare it to the face of an owl. It dominates the village, its vast shadow hanging over every building from approximately ten A.M. to four P.M. More often than not, even in the height of summer, the mountain wears a cap of snow. From its foot to its middle, straddling it like a girdle, there's a forest of silver birch and oak.

Was a forest.

As you stand, still stunned, at your bedroom window, putting on your school uniform, you notice something you'd missed earlier. Trees scattered along the edge of the road, their trunks torn, branches stamped flat.

It looks as if the mountain walked away.

*

Have you looked outside, Dad?

What?

Have you looked outside?

Can't you see I've got things to do, Frankie? I'm making a cup of tea for Angela, sorting your brother's bag, putting on a wash, and trying to get ready for work. I've got a phone call with my bloody editor at eight-thirty, I can't be late and I'm not—

The mountain's gone.

What?

The mountain . . . it's not there anymore.

Very funny.

I'm not joking.

He frowns, a smear of Marmite on his beard. Dad is always doing something else while he eats, reading or checking his phone. Food rarely holds his attention. Often, you are the one to let him know, tip him the wink. But now you ignore it, point to the window.

Look. Outside.

*

The school is on the east side of the village but you head west.

You run as fast as you can. You hate being late but can't resist taking a closer look. When you reach the car park, you discover you're no longer the only one who has noted the sizable absence.

There are a pair of irate German hikers who wear bright technical clothing and are stabbing at their smart phones in perplexity. Charlotte, the village's yoga instructor ('Vinyasa Flow every Tuesday and Thursday at 10 A.M. in the community centre, £5 a session'), sways and rotates her wrists, cheeks wet with tears. There are a few others you recognise sat in their cars, shy smirks on their faces, as if they are expecting a camera crew or an unknown celebrity to leap out and shout 'surprise'.

The only person who seems completely unaffected by the monumental vanishing is the community traffic warden, who continues clockwise around the car park, lifting his camera, taking note of the arrival of each vehicle in meticulous detail, slotting tickets neatly under windscreen wipers.

You attempt to take in the vast hole in the landscape. It's too much. Panic, uncertainty, confusion. You wobble in your trainers.

There's a small, round shard of stone on the ground. It's clearly an orphan rock, lost when the mountain left. You pick it up. It's surprisingly heavy and very warm, as if it has recently been removed from a fire.

As you hear the faint tinkle of the school bell in the distance, the German hikers head out of the car park in their BMW, muttering polysyllabic curses under their breaths.

You drop the stone into your pocket and set off at a run.

*

A memory. You don't say where you're going. Hardly anyone local ever visits the mountain. It's the last place they'd expect you to go.

You've had a fight with your little brother, a minor thing, a broken pen, but it has led you to be banished to your bedroom. Again. It's a constant fact that you'll always take the fall for any row with your younger sibling. Since Mum died, your dad is unwavering in his assertion that you must always take the high ground, set an example. This time you give in without a word. You close the door firmly, wait a few minutes, before slipping out of your window and heading off uphill.

The mountain enfolds you. You haven't gone very far before the house and the village become smudges beneath your heel. You pass through the forest, noting the way in which the tiny, glittering silver birch leaves wave like small hands in the breeze, encouraging and playful. Each step takes you to a new air, to a clearer sense of yourself and a world that is fresh and unexpected. You reach the top of the tree line. Civilisation has vanished. Around and above, there's only rock and sky and light.

*

The school corridors are full of chat and buzz about the missing mountain but no-one talks to you until Cleo sends a text in Higher Maths.

My mum reckons it's the Chinese.

Cleo and her mum are magnets for conspiracy. They live in a semi on the edge of the village, surrounded by dogs, tinned food and a library of outlandish literature from dubious American publishers. Cleo's dad died of a heart attack while working on the submarines but she tells everyone he was executed as a spy by the government. She has a ready-made story for any disaster, a random fantasy that she declares with such conviction that she has a reliable gang of fanatics who hang on her every word.

You're fairly certain that Cleo has sent the same text to the whole class but reply and to your surprise another text appears almost at once.

My mum says that mountains are sacred in China. She says that only the Chinese have the technology to pull off something so epic.

You type the words: *your mum is a racist* but delete them. Cleo clearly senses your scepticism.

Personally I think it's a stunt.

You respond with a question mark.

Cleo replies so fast it's impossible to believe she hadn't got her answer pre-planned.

Like by a famous person. Like when Kanye went for President to promote his new album.

Mr Taylor is talking about quadratic equations. He seems oblivious, not noticing that every student in the class either has their head tilted towards their phone or is chatting openly with their neighbour. His voice has the tone of a tired fly, smacking lightly against a closed window.

You type the thing that has been bothering you: *but why my mountain?*

You stare at your phone for a moment then over to Cleo. She's whispering to Justin and the message remains unread. You drop your phone into your bag, pick up your pen and start scribbling on your notepad.

My mountain. My mountain. My mountain. My mountain. My mountain. My

*

Since when is it your mountain?

Until you write the words, there's never been a moment when you have claimed ownership over the mountain, not even in your mind. Yet to your surprise, its absence has created an equal void within you.

You lose time.

There are whole hours spent staring out the window at the sky. No, not the sky. The place in the sky where the mountain used to be.

The emptiness.

You stare at the emptiness and wonder what – if anything – could possibly fill it.

*

That Friday evening, you're sat outside the pub on one of the picnic tables with a sparkling water and two packets of salt-and-vinegar crisps. One for you, the other a decoy packet for Angus the dog who munches angrily at your feet.

It's late but the sun is still high in the sky. There are a few more weeks of long summer days yet to come. Everything has a bright edge but the shadows are long.

Your little brother plays an improvised game of shinty in the meadow with the Brodie girls, using a bit of old fence for sticks and a crushed can of Irn-Bru as the ball.

It's been a disorientating few days. You've not been yourself. There's a heaviness in your chest, a weight pressing down, a sadness that has been impossible to shake off. You're slow to move. You've spent a lot of every day curled up on the sofa, silent and staring at nothing in particular. It took everything you had to come along tonight.

You have your back to the emptiness, facing instead the open windows of the pub listening to the myriad arguments, points and counterpoints, and other random Highland musings.

fairy magic . . . police say it's not their business . . . army need to . . . bonfires are the problem . . . my granny always swore we were descended from trolls . . . where are the council . . . fucking tourists . . . laws of physics isn't it . . .

The landlord, also called Angus (he is Big Angus, the dog is Wee Angus) is a local councillor. Any time there's an issue in the village, everyone comes to the pub. It's the only time people congregate except for shinty matches. Dad's girlfriend, Angela, dragged him along and because your little brother refuses to be babysat by you, it became a family affair.

 . . . part of village identity . . . Sassenach conspiracy . . . eyesore . . . where me and Jack first, you know, wink wink, nudge nudge . . . geological breakdown . . . aye but development opportnities . . . housing . . . forestry manager was on the phone with the MP . . . where will the butterfly club meet, eh . . . loss of face . . . telling you, it's the fucking English government . . . magic trick, surely, David Copperface or whatever . . . it'll come back when it's hungry . . .

A cold, wet hardness on your leg. Wee Angus has finished his crisps, his long snout jabbing insistently on your thigh. You don't want any trouble – he's been known to bite even the most generous tourists – so you drop the rest of your packet onto the ground where it is swiftly devoured.

As far as you can make out from the discussion inside, the mountain's disappearance seems to be a unique event. There have been no other geological abnormalities in the region. There are arguments about what should be done. Some people talk about starting an online petition, others about keeping the whole thing quiet, hoping no-one will notice and gently deleting all mention of the mountain in local records. There's some surprise that it hasn't been mentioned in local news. Alan, the local policeman and skipper of the shinty team, says there's nothing in the criminal code regarding the loss of such a sizable edifice.

The evening wears on, the sun refusing to set, but the debate falters once Big Angus brings out his famously lethal self-brewed IPA, handing out free pints to everyone, even a half to each child. You take one gulp and quickly run to the bins to vomit.

The world spins on its axis. You lie down on the gravel, letting the rough edges of the tiny rocks dig into your skin. A bead of blood pops on your chin. You hope the pain will wake you from this nightmare.

But by the next morning, everyone in the village will have a sore head and, for all intents and purposes, the matter of the missing mountain will be forgotten.

*

The mountain is in your bedroom. You don't ask yourself how this is possible, it just is. You're not asleep but keep your eyes closed. You have a sense that if you open your eyes, the mountain will vanish. It fills every available space. You can feel its mossy boulders pressing against your toes. The sharp edge of a cliff top nestles into your hair. The surface of the lochan ripples gently like a wildcat breathing.

It's watching you.

You feel encased in its gaze. Like it is trying to work out if it can trust you.

The mountain is in your bedroom, watching, silent for a long time until eventually it begins to speak.

It speaks in landslide, rock fall, boulder roll, a vibrating cacophony of smashing, splintering, yawing, crumbling, breaking, a scream lodges in your throat but even if you were able to open your mouth you doubt whether you'd be heard, and you cling to the duvet, head wedged tightly to the pillow, toes clamped to the bedframe. As hard as you try to focus on the beats and shatters of its tongue, you cannot make out what it is saying. You wish you could ask it to slow down, explain, draw a picture. It's impossible. The space between you and it, between words and meaning, feels like a galaxy. The mountain's tone is terrible, mournful, desolate: that much you can tell. The longer you listen, the sadder you feel, the heavier your heart. It hurts to listen. The sadness of the mountain, its awful keening.

Eventually you reach out a hand, open your eyes and—

*

You're awake. The bedroom is empty. There's no mountain. Only the echo of its wail ringing in your ears. You sit up, wipe your eyes of sleep, and notice the orphan rock from the car park sitting on your bedside table.

In the early morning light, it appears to be gently pulsing.

*

It doesn't take long for an inch of wild grass to fill the space where the mountain once lay. The ground is scarred, brutalised like a layer of exposed muscle but, after a week or so, the raw red tone begins to fade.

Everyone in the village is a little dazed by the extra light. It's September now but days are still long. Without the mountain's constant shadow, the intensity of village life increases. Tempers fray. Mrs Donaldson who met Mr Donaldson on the south-west pass shortly after finishing her nurse's exams in 2002, takes the hint, and finally leaves after two decades of disappointment. Jock Tarbet, the owner of the 'Mountain View B&B', loses his temper at a meeting of the Parish Council and is last seen hitchhiking on the northbound side of the main road. A fight breaks out in the car park between rival bus tour operators, the drivers coming to blows beside the disabled toilets of the visitor centre, each believing that the mountain's vanishing to be yet another feint in their endless game of one-upmanship. There's a sense that the village has become disconnected from its mooring.

It's loose.

Floats.

Without the mountain, the village is in danger of drifting off down the glen.

Nature is similarly confounded by the loss. A family of deer are filmed entering the community centre, refusing to leave the café area, eating the flowers in the vases, their internal map torn in two. The video goes viral. Frogs explode in the extra sunshine. There are many reports of birds, those that would normally seek high shelter in the mountain's caves and crevices, nesting on the ground.

You continue to experience a sense of disorientation. The village is composed of three meandering but parallel roads so it's impossible to get lost yet on more than one occasion you find yourself at the wrong end of Station Road.

Without the obvious landmark, you are bewildered.

Patrick James Errington
MISSIVE

Watching, silent, another storm gather
along a far lip of hill, hesitate, then spill

over into the valley. Night somewhere,
coming swiftly. And something coming

little by little loose in me. A door left
unlatched. A word I can so nearly

recall . . .   Windows stutter against
their frames. *You*. It must be. Or what I

still call *you*. That slight gap in the endless,
perfect elsewhere.
                    Rain beginning again, light

for now. Wind filling the chimney like a deep
breath. As though about to sigh, or speak out.

CALLING A WOLF A WOLF

Come on, out with it, my father calls over his shoulder, over
his breath, barks it, breaking off the words like dead

twigs – *Spit it out* – like the action figure I'm holding broken.
Tell it like it is. Like it is. Me, shaking there, six and sparrow

in the hawk of him, in the shadow of the garage he always
seems to be fixing. Silence a hand over my mouth. I want nothing

like it is. I want the blood that will, later, billow blue
beneath my left eye like stormclouds. I want his hands,

even now, want wind-bent wheat, my body antlered with light.
I want that morning, not any of the others, want some kind of

kindness, air swollen with storm, snow that won't
come, that never comes. *Come on, boy,* he calls me

like a dog. But something else steps softly from the storm.

Jane Flett
DON'T FORGET TO BREATHE

Barring the unlikely event of a lottery win or revolution, in three days Andriy Melnyk will load twenty-five dolphins, six walruses, three sea lions, and a white beluga whale onto a Russian transport aircraft to fly from Sevastopol to the Persian Gulf.

He'll accompany them for the journey and, after making sure they've settled into their new life in Iran, Andriy will come home to Ukraine to start the next part of his life. The money from their sale might save him, it's true, though he can barely think about that now. It's the customs declarations he's most dreading. That, and the moment he has to stand alone, back in the hangar in Sevastopol, listening out for a squeal and chatter that will never arrive.

He's been keeping busy as much as he can over the past week: disinfecting the empty tanks, closing up the expense accounts, making gingerbread men. Actually, entire gingerbread civilisations: once Andriy gets going, he's no good at reining in his enthusiasm. His last Sunday baking session ended up with entire family trees dating back to the Bolsheviks. Mascha tells him it's a waste of resources, but flour is the one thing they're *not* short of, and the ginger's still thriving in the garden where Katrya planted it before everything went to shit.

Admittedly, they're not as sweet as the ones Baba used to make, but no one's eating them anyway. They're hard as rocks, and there's something unsettling about the faces: a too-keenness maybe, an enthusiasm that doesn't befit creatures whose only destiny is to be masticated to death. Still, Andriy can't bear to throw them away, so he squirrels them instead, filling up cupboards and boxes and drawers, before returning to the kitchen to start another batch.

He'd rather not look at them once he's done, their grins stretched wide by his own thumbs, but he can't quit either, these small petty comforts of working the dough.

Still, it's the least of his worries. He's pretty sure that Mascha goes through the drawers when she thinks he's not paying attention, filling up plastic bags with whole families and throwing them in the trash. He's aware his daughter thinks he's got a screw loose and is dealing with it the only way she can, though this doesn't stop him from judging her methods. It's unnecessary. And foolish – who can tell when the next hungers will come, when the gingerbread men will offer them salvation?

He's never quite sure how he and Katrya added up to produce a girl like Mascha. She is smart, efficient – ruthless as a torpedo. And then there's Katrya, who is all soft edges, and giggles when she shakes people's hands. It is like mixing cotton and sugar and coming up with iron. Or like flour and water and coming up with these rock hard men.

Perhaps he used to be like that. It's true, he once trained three of his best dolphins – Astran, Seriy, and Belka – for the greatest mission. The kamikaze mission. Strap a mine to their forehead and send them off to get on nodding acquaintance with the hull of an enemy ship.

Kaboom: this shipping route is CLOSED.

The hardest part was teaching them the difference between foreign and Soviet submarines. Below the water, all shadows are the same colour, and there's no explaining the subtle differences of Russian ship names to the dolphins. Even he has a hard time keeping up: is it admirals for the battleships and animals for the submarines? Or the other way round? Eventually, he worked it out though. It was the sound of the propellers that told them apart.

It had been a beautiful breakthrough. Something had clicked within Astran and she had flung her body, again and again, to the correct dummy float of the training area, barely pausing for a flicker of the tail. And once she'd got it, the other two fell like dominoes and the celebrations that night had been an endless fountain of chum and whooping.

It was a double-edged sword, of course, because the better the dolphins were at finding the hull, the more likely it was that they were never coming back. Andriy has never let himself think about this too hard – has never, for that matter, considered what he was doing to be military training. If anything, he viewed himself as more like a military mother, preparing his children the best he could for the harsh realities of the outside world. No one blames the mother if her boys don't come home; everyone knows she's the one who suffers the most.

Andriy has not yet had to face this particular reality, and who knows what will become of his dolphins in Iran, what use they will have for them? Either way, he's convinced it will be he who sheds the most tears after Friday, he whose heart breaks when he steps back on the plane and flies back, alone.

*

Andriy arrives at the aquarium a little before six A.M. It's his favourite time to start training – when the grey morning light spills through the windows and the dolphins get to be his first conversations of the day.

He used to do this when Katrya was still at home too. Used to slip out of bed before dawn and shuffle down the stairs, pulling on his trousers in the corridor so as not to wake her – a gesture that was cloaked in sympathy for her need to sleep, but also, if he is honest, one that came from a deep desire to begin the day without a single conversation with his wife.

Some people think training means sharp sticks and loud voices, but it doesn't work like that. Dolphins don't understand negative reinforcement, never have. The correct way – the way Andriy trained *his* animals – is to react to any mistakes with the three second pause. The Least Reinforcing Stimulus, or LRS for those in the business. Not that there are many others in the business any more, but still. A short time out, and then you try again.

It's not that hitting would be cruel. On the contrary – for a dolphin, *any* attention is worth it. An electric shock or a smack to the flank is its own reward and they'll keep on pressing the pellet, even as you keep trying to prove to them they're making the wrong choice. You can't out-smack a dolphin, and this is why, as the joke went, all the American military dolphins ended up dead.

Andriy had never understood why this was the case – hadn't understood it with Katrya either, for that matter, when she'd first brought up the idea in bed. He'd watched the films on her request though, and she'd laughed, at first, at the way he winced when the mechanic wrapped his thick fist around the woman's neck, as her own hands spasmed, pink plastic nails flailing. There'd been something desperate in that laugh, he realises now. Because it wasn't funny. It was horrible, and she had known it was horrible, and when she'd asked him to do it anyway, she was asking them to hold hands in this horribleness and let it wash over them, like tides across pebbles, while they stared out to sea.

Or maybe not. Maybe she'd meant it when she said it was just some fun, and perhaps it is exactly that fun that she is having now, with Matryk the locksmith, and everything his daughter has ever told him about being too literal, too old-fashioned, is the truth.

*

The moment he opens the door to the aquarium, the dolphins start to squeal and thrash their bodies up and down in the water. To the untrained ear, it sounds like white noise but in fact each dolphin has its own very particular call – a signature whistle that marks them out as individuals. The dolphin fingerprint, if you will.

Andriy tells dolphin facts to anyone who'll listen, and a few who won't. It was how he'd first made conversation with Katrya, in fact, thirty-six years ago in Peytroyska's bar, over stale beers and shots of horilka.

He'd been charmed by the way she sat smack in the middle of the barstool, her stubby legs kicking the air like a child and, later, by the single tooth that jutted out against her lower lip, so that she permanently seemed to be just on the verge of spilling some secret.

Dolphins have to remind themselves to breathe, he'd told her, and that's why when they sleep, they only ever let half their brain rest at a time. If they let their whole self fall unconscious, they'd forget to inhale, and they'd die.

Not me, she'd laughed, downing the rest of her horilka and slamming the glass against the wet table. When I conk out, I'm out for the night.

Andriy can barely believe that he was ever so confident to answer the way he had. But he had, and it had worked, for they had gone home together that night, and spent every night together for the next week, and their marriage had slipped into place, the way a snib does, and held them both tight.

It hadn't been a wild courtship but, if Andriy is honest, he hadn't minded that. In fact, if Andriy is very honest, wildness is not something that he has ever viewed as an option, as something that could be missing from his relationship, or indeed his life.

Except, perhaps, on two occasions. The first being the day Katrya left, the day she told him they couldn't keep up this charade any more, that they had to stop pretending. The day he had agreed, too embarrassed to admit that he hadn't been pretending, what did she think he was pretending about? Until later he worked it out. She had meant *she*, not they. He hadn't been pretending after all.

The other time was two summers ago, during a training session in the Black Sea. He'd sent five spy dolphins out on an exercise, and only two had come back. They'd held the ship, waiting, sent out a dozen different whistle noises, turned the sea around the boat crimson with chum. Nothing. Eventually, as the sky had turned the same angry grey-black as the water, they had turned back, leaving the three dolphins, abandoning them to the twisting corridors that wound their way deep beneath the ocean. Lost, perhaps, in an endless inky night. Waiting, surely, for Andriy's rescue.

Arkady, the ship's engineer, who considered himself an expert on these things, had tried to console. It's mating season. They're just excited, they're following their animal instincts. Don't worry, they'll be back.

And so they were, ten days later and barely changed for the experience, apart from Astran, who'd picked up a souvenir from her trip in the form of a calf, and had to be taken off bomb duty for the rest of her pregnancy. It had hurt Andriy, just a little, that for all the hours they'd spent going over the drills, the dolphins were willing to abandon him in an instant for hot thrash of flesh.

It was their animal instincts. Of course. But still.

Andriy doesn't blame them for being taken over by a fit of passion – doesn't blame Katrya either, for that matter – but there's a part of him that can't help feeling that the whole idea of this fit is a cheap fabrication, an excuse pasted onto a decision after the fact. He's not sure he believes in animal instincts, if he's honest. He's seen enough instances of wilful choices, the pause before the follow-through.

*

Astran is the one he's most worried about now, the one who is making this decision a dozen times more difficult than it could be. In the last months she's been getting sicker, her fin mottled with shallow pock marks like acne, and it's been a week since the last of the medicine ran out. There's no money to buy more – there's not even money for fish or food supplements. Sooner or later they're going to have to switch off the water purifiers. Sooner, rather than later, there's going to be nothing left in the bucket to throw. He has been terrified for weeks that one day he will come down to the aquarium to find one of them floating on the surface like a huge bloated goldfish, and whenever he unlocks the door and steps up to the tank, it takes every ounce of willpower to hold his head up and look, really look, at where he is going.

*

Andriy is not an idiot. He knows what people have been saying, that there are plenty who think he's contributing to some fundamental global instability. The official line is that the Iranian government have built a new oceanarium, just to his specifications, where tourists can flock from far and wide to see the dolphins perform, all the while continuing the research. The important scientific research. The official line is that this particular dolphin training has marked an important leap forward in animal psychology, and it would be a crime to abandon the progress that's been made.

It's not fooling anyone, least of all Mascha, who tells him she'd be horrified if she had any horror left to spare, which she doesn't. The trip has gone onto the long list of things he doesn't talk about with his daughter, along with his baking habits, the future, and the reasons behind their divorce. For this, he is grateful.

When he thinks about the last months with Katrya now, it's obvious, of course, that things weren't right. And yet, he is still convinced that when he was in the moment, there was no part of him that was pretending. Perhaps it is like those Impressionistic painters Mascha is always talking about, who make sense from a distance but up close are just thick wild swirls of colour.

She had asked him just to try it, just once, to hit her in the face while they were making love, and he had got to the moment of drawing his hand back before he broke down.

'I can't,' he'd said. 'I'm sorry, *kohana*. I'm just not the kind of man who can hit his wife.'

'This isn't about you,' she'd said, and that was the moment she'd started to cry. 'Don't you get it?'

'Katrya,' he'd said. It would be the last time they'd ever sleep together.

'You keep saying you don't want to hurt me,' she'd said, wiping a trail of mucus on the back of her arm. 'But you're killing me, Andriy. This here? Is killing me.'

*

There is another option, which is to open the gate now, take the boat out, and lead the animals to open water. To wait for their instincts to take over. Even a year ago, he would have considered this.

Now? They would not survive, none of them. Or maybe a sea lion or two, the sea lions being the quickest to train but even quicker to revert to their own ways the moment you stop. The dolphins do not stand a chance. He has tainted them, the way you can taint a baby bird by trying to help it back to the nest, so the mother will always smell your sweaty palms on its feathers and let it starve.

Still, perhaps he is wrong about this. It is possible – he has been wrong about so many things. Who knows? The wildness could still be within them, waiting for the right moment to unleash.

Andriy stands at the railing, clenching it with both hands, and watches the dolphins arc and dash in the water. There's a tightness lodged in his throat like a bright red beachball and, when he leans forward, his keyring clatters against the rail. It's okay, he reminds himself. Andriy forces himself to look, to really look, at the creatures suspended in the pure blue water. He closes his eyes and takes a deep breath: consciously, all the way down.

Ewan Forbes
'MAN WHO HAS JUST SHOT HIMSELF' –
LEWIS, CARSTON (2021)

A man walks into a gallery. He places a small plaque on the wall behind him. It says *'Man Who Has Just Shot Himself' – Lewis, Carston (2021)*, and it looks just like all the plaques next to all the other pieces in the gallery. The only other patron in the room does not notice him place it.

That art lover, after peering at a Hirst with a disgruntled look on his pale-skinned face, wraps himself in an overly long scarf, and leaves.

The first man, the man who placed the plaque on the bare white wall, pulls a gun from a leather satchel he wears over his shoulder. From his deep jacket pocket he pulls a silencer and affixes it to the gun.

He puts the gun in his mouth.

He pulls the trigger.

Ten minutes later two other patrons walk by, pausing by the body in the pool of blood on the way to the Hirst.

'Visceral,' says one.

'Kitsch,' says the other.

*

Neither patron read the report in the news the next day of what exactly they had provided single-word assessments of, nor did they, either of them, recall the experience in the particular ever again. It would be mentioned in their company a year later, and they both of them feigned the kind of shock that they deemed appropriate, before moving the discussion on to the Hirst they had seen at 'around about the same time'.

The story was mentioned in local newspapers, and in one national, but barely at all online. It happened the same week the politician who nobody seemed to have heard of before accidentally publicly posted a picture of his penis on social media. The story of Carston Lewis's demise was the sort of thing that was mentioned at dinner to prompt shock and a shake of the head, or in the office, sometimes along with a gruesome and entirely fictional elaboration presented as fact. It would have died there, passed over in conversation by a dog that could play Jenga long enough to film it for ninety seconds, or perhaps by the overinflated media response to the return of a fast-food product. But it didn't. Instead, it happened again.

*

Two years to the day later, Lewis Carston walks into a gallery. He places a small plaque on the wall behind him. It says *Man Who Has Just Shot Himself'* – *Carston, Lewis (2023)* and it looks just like all the plaques next to all the other pieces in the gallery. There is no other patron in the room to notice him place it.

The CCTV camera looked on so that later commentators could say that he looked determined. On television, two art historians would glibly report the effort as kitsch, though both would at least admit that it was visceral. They even looked like the patrons mentioned earlier. These are coincidences, nothing more.

It was not, initially at least, considered coincidental that Lewis Carston had such a similar name to Carston Lewis. It was assumed by the press and the public that Mr Carston had taken his inspiration from Mr Lewis, though later investigation would reveal no direct links, or even apparent awareness of the previous incident on the part of Mr Carston. While Lewis was a failed artist, Carston was not. A butcher by trade, he was by all accounts a happy and fulfilled family man, putting him once again distinct from the single and struggling Mr Lewis. His family reported that they could not recall him being particularly interested in art. Nonetheless, the connection was hard to shake for as long as the story was news.

*

Two years later, a second Lewis Carston would enter a small gallery in Minsk, the *Mastackaje Dziarmo*. The plaque he placed on the wall did not look dissimilar to all the plaques next to all the other pieces in the gallery, though it was in English and not Belarusian. It said *'Man Who Has Just Shot Himself'* – *Carston, Lewis (2025)*. There were three other patrons of the gallery in the room at the time.

Afterwards, there was some debate as to whether or not the Second Mr Carston had understood the rules that dictate that forenames should be preceded by surnames on plaques such as these. Hinging on this vital piece of information, there was a debate in the art world regarding the intent of the Second Mr Carston. Had he been paying tribute to the original piece by Carston Lewis, the second by Lewis Carston (no relation), or had he in fact been doing something new in what might be an evolving work that would include many artists? Without this knowledge, no-one was so gauche as to accuse the Second Mr Carston of engaging in kitsch, and the photos of the three other patrons who witnessed the event, speaking a thousand words each in shades of crimson, left assessments of the visceral unneeded.

The Second Mr Carston had been an American tourist, a Bostonian by birth. As a foreign-language teacher, he had spent the preceding years in South-East Asia, to which he had left no ties. His lone living family member, a retired church minister, was senile, and could shed no light on his grandson's actions. His online footprint gave no indication as to what he had been about to do, revealed only a passing interest in art, and yielded no posts on either Lewis or the original Carston.

*

The story was now international. Taxi drivers would speculate with their riders as to whether or not it would happen again. Barbers would ask their clients where they thought it would happen next, which segued nicely into questions about holidays without too many conversational acrobatics. There were think-pieces aplenty on the individual motives of the three men, and, with a numbing inevitability, abstracted explanations of what it meant to live in a world where such a thing was happening.

When 2026 eventually arrived, there was an anticipation of a continuation of the Carston Lewis phenomenon. Much ink and billions of black pixels were dedicated to threadbare profiles of Lewis, the two Carstons, and their supposed intentions: all of it speculative conjecture. Galleries announced that they would have extra security when the anniversary of the original act arrived. Staffing was increased for galleries in general to contend with the expected attendance bump that had much more to do with ghoulish curiosity and a lack of commitment to personal safety than it did any love of the arts.

It was late March, several months earlier than expected, when a man known as Louis Carson strapped several pounds of explosive and numerous packs of paint to his person before taking part in a speed graffiti competition in Aurora, Illinois. One of the competition's judges would later say that the young Carson had stood stock still as the timer had started and the other competitors had jumped into action. It was only as one of them looked like they were nearing completion that he had removed a small plaque from his pocket before affixing it carefully to the wall in front of him.

Footage retrieved from an onlooker's phone would later show the young man pulling a rectangular sheet of metal from his pocket to hold in front of the plaque, shielding it from the blast. The explosion critically injured one of the other competitors, and several onlookers had to receive medical attention. The news teams that arrived to cover the story took special care to document Carson's work. The spray of blood and paint covered the efforts of the other competitors completely, a violent consumption of space in blood red, white, blue, textured by organ tissue. No prize was issued, no winner declared.

The choice of red, white, and blue, and the nationalist evocation they inspire, went mostly unremarked upon. It is not that the fact did not fit the narrative, so much as it is easy to ignore as a one-off when there was so much more to mention, in a culture in which distractions from such conversations were harder to come by. As with any news event, and unlike the work of our young graffiti artist, it is generally, and mostly silently, agreed that the picture painted need not be 'guts and all'.

It transpired in the coverage that followed that Louis Carson had his name legally changed to Carston in the weeks leading up to the competition. Curiously, and despite this effort, he had used his original name when making his plaque: 'Man Who Has Just Shot Himself' – Carson, Louis (2026). His mother said that he'd never shown any indication of what was to come; his girlfriend reported that they had a trip organised together in the coming weeks. When asked, neither had the slightest clue where he had procured the explosives.

There was now little doubt as the actual anniversary approached that there would be more days such as these. There were many theories, but they were based on little-to-no evidence. The now four contributors to the Lewis, Carston project all seemed completely unconnected to one another. Two Americans, two Brits, over three countries, and, with the latest work in the sequence opening up the options, or rather, new methods of execution. These facts formed the foundations of the speculation, and as such their predictive power was limited. In every iteration of the very similar articles that discussed the subject, there was a hope that in the climate of awareness someone would be caught in the act.

In the days preceding, journalists hunted down as many Carstons as they could. There were not many. The name is from Old English and means 'free peasant settlement', making its lack of popularity as a first name unsurprising. The largest concentration was to be found in the United States, where, at least nominally divorced from class or history, names mean little if anything. None of the men tracked down had much to say, and none of them went on to commit art.

In the end the journalists' search proved short-sighted. The further four successful Carstons of 2026 did not share a name with any of the previous Carstons. Named Holger Kunst, Lu Rui, Andre Girard, and Stephen Baxter, only one of them, Baxter, a Brit, shared a nationality with any of his predecessors. They came from distinct walks of life: Kunst was a successful banker, Lu a pilot, Girard a clown, and Baxter a nurse. Of the four, only Girard had a known interest in art, and of the Carstons in particular; he was on record as saying that he suspected that Carston Lewis must have, himself, been a clown. Lu was visiting family, who had missed him at a BBQ that afternoon. Baxter had left work earlier that day complaining of a stomach bug. The day before placing his plaque, Kunst had purchased tickets so that he and his brother could travel the Trans-Siberian Express (later, when his estate was being dealt with, it was discovered that Kunst, who lived alone, owned the world's largest train set, a whole sprawling town and country, though that is neither here nor there – of note, perhaps, it did contain a miniature replica of an art gallery).

All four men had placed plaques that stated that they were Carston Lewis. Of the four, only Girard, a purist, would buck the trend of using the current year, opting instead for 2021. Three of the men used handguns to achieve their ends. Kunst used a grenade that had lived on his desk at work for as long as anyone could remember, an object that had been understood until that moment to be a deactivated reminder of his paternal grandfather's war crimes.

Of the would-be artists who did not succeed, an elderly Japanese woman was the only one available for comment. This was unfortunate, as she did so in Japanese to a confused and monolingual Lebanese journalist who was without recording equipment. Two others had failed to operate their weapons appropriately, one through a struggle with a security guard and the other through ineptitude. They were taken to intensive care units, where they both later died. None of the three of them had placed their plaques. This had become, without anyone arguing the case or really noticing at the time, the official stamp of inclusion in the pantheon of Lewis, Carston, and nobody saw fit to question the logic.

*

In 1774, Goethe's novel *Die Leiden des jungen Werthers* (*The Sorrows of Young Werther*) had two prominent features that would come to take hold of the imagination of the reading public: a class of young men who wore yellow trousers with blue jackets, and suicide by pistol. Within months of the book's publication, life had imitated art on both questionable fronts. The first would leave with the fashions of the day. These were slow enough to have cost a good several men the attention of young women more attracted to partners with an eye for proper attire than those with a suggestible mind and an appreciation of literature. The second would go on to become such a recognisable pattern of copycat behaviour that it would later find itself named the Werther Effect.

Rene Girard (no relation to our clown) argued that all desire is memetic, that we have to see something modelled before we can want it. This is something the advertising industry understands well, the general public less so. The Werther Effect suggests that we can learn to desire a dramatic release from the cage of mere existence in much the same way we can learn to desire sausages (if not, for obvious reasons, to the same degree). We are, more often than not, unlike the romantic young Werner, or the little known but much acknowledged artist trailblazer Lewis. The maths does not play in our favour.

'Man is the creature who does not know what to desire'. The argument goes that he must have his desires showcased. Perhaps the artistic death drive of the Lewis, Carstons was a last-ditch effort of those who had privately and internally despaired until they had seen a way out that suggested meaning where they themselves, until then, had seen none. This view comprised the dominant media narrative. In this world, Girard's words give some sort of reassurance, even if only as a comforting nod to some underlying order of things. But as memetic as the phenomenon became, the more investigation the early incidents were subjected to, the more it seemed that there was nothing to connect them. The first three men had no relationship to each other, no shared motive or appreciation of the arts, or, it seemed to anyone who cared to look, awareness that they were to be taking part in something larger. But the idea that all the similarities were mere chance was too much for anyone to bear. Much more comforting, ironically, to believe that these events were products of a shared despair than macabre fortuitousness. The universal is for the most part a collectivising force, whereas the particular has too much of a tendency to stray into oddness, weirdness, or pariahdom. Better to believe in a shared fear of a lack of a future or something of that nature. After all, we'll believe there's no future for many years to come. It is cosier and more comforting to imagine that we can discern ourselves in the actions of the mad or unhinged, to imagine our own pressures playing out in a dramatic and compelling conclusion. It saves us from acknowledging the banality of our lives, the pointlessness of most of our worries, but also, perhaps, acts as a subconscious defence against allowing our minds to fall into the same destructive patterns that took life from those we picture ourselves empathising with. But sympathy is not empathy, and considering action without insight is like watching the surface of a dark lake. The movements tell you more about the surroundings, the wind, the weather, than they do anything beneath the surface.

As an event unfolds, and different people are woven into it, the meaning, if there ever was one, becomes diffuse. It stands in our memory, if at all, alongside politicians who accidentally posted pictures of their privates online, dogs that can play Jenga, and whatever we were going through at the time. Even if we can focus, why it started is painted over by the layers of complexity that are added with each new participant, each new variation. People see what they want to see, and allow events to be coloured and shaped in their minds by the other unconnected events of the day, and by the views of others, and by the fullness of their stomach upon receiving new information, as well as a screaming multitude of other factors beyond their comprehension, yours, or mine. The cultural echoes of unvoiced action manifest differently than those with a vocal champion, and a true mystery will always be traced back to a voice that remains stubbornly (and usually cadaverously) silent. Perhaps, if we're lucky, the voice's owner will leave a plaque or marker of some kind to mark the fact that a mystery exists at all.

Helena Fornells
THE FALL

on the boat   with a brother
with a father   on the sea
in the sea   rock below brother
on the island   a tower and trees
from the woods   to the sand
with the boat   on the beach
from the tower   to the father
after the father   towards the sea
dark green woodlands   on the island
with a fire   on the beach
a few branches   under the father
on the boat   with a machine
made of wood   towards the island
from the tower   to the trees
after a red ladder   a father
heavy rain   under the trees
with a knife   towards a father
with a brother   to the beach
iron ladder   up the tower
on the island   with one fish
an iron boat   and a rowboat
chopping wood   from the trees
in the night   on the island
on the beach   with the father
on the rowboat   with a body
            with his body
            in the sea

Sally Gales
BIRTHDAY WISHES

Death ruined my birthday. Of course, I know it ruined everyone else's. And I know I shouldn't complain. I shouldn't even be counting birthdays anymore. I turned one hundred and three today.

I walked to the shop to pick up my usuals: a loaf of bread, few tins of fruit, sliced chicken, and a handful of ready meals – only pasta, the others give me the boke. At the counter, I threw in a small Dairy Milk as a celebratory treat.

Alice raised an eyebrow.

Secretly I hoped she would give me a sign that she remembered. A wink. A discount. Even a nod. But, of course, she only thought of today's *other* commemorated event.

'You going tonight?'

I sighed and took my chocolate from her hand. 'You know I am, Alice.'

'Yes, but is your name in for the Draw?'

I packed my groceries, stretching up to reach a tin of peaches Alice hadn't pushed to the edge of the counter. My fingers just failed to reach the can.

'Oh, sorry about that, Mini.'

I despised that nickname. I was short. It wasn't clever.

Alice pushed the tin towards me. I tried to take it but she held on and leaned forward. Her long sand-coloured hair was pulled back and a hint of shadow flashed from the edge of her shirt. I was sure she had intentionally left those top buttons undone. Some people had all the luck. Sixteen forever . . .

'So, are you?' she asked.

I pulled the tin out of her grasp and shoved it in my bag, momentarily forgetting the loaf of bread, until I heard its plastic crinkle of protest. I flinched.

'Good-bye, Alice.'

My curt response did not have the desired effect. 'Oh, Mini. You always loved to keep your secrets. That's fine. I'll see you later tonight.'

I had kept a secret from her one time. The year before I turned thirteen. I didn't want to tell her the song I had chosen for the talent show. She could remember that but not my birthday. Alice's laugh followed me out the door.

*

My thirteenth birthday party had been at the local pool. Adjacent to the cliffs that ran along our town, I had bugged my mum for months. She had tried to convince me otherwise.

'Your birthday is in the middle of March.'

'What if winter isn't over by the time it comes?'

'You know March always brings a lot of rain.'

I had refused to listen to her naysaying and in the end, she caved.

'Fine. But I can't get my deposit back. You will have to sit at the pool for four hours – no matter what.'

When she later asked me what kind of cake I wanted her to make, I hesitated. In the past, I had usually alternated between an all-chocolate number or vanilla sponge with chocolate frosting, but that year was special. I was growing up. I had just bought my very first two-piece bathing suit. I decided to go for a tropical theme, ideal for a poolside event.

The night before my birthday, the smell of burnt coconut filled my home.

*

'Hey, Mini!'

I took the last few steps up the hill at the edge of town before turning. All those years of living in the same place and I never had managed to get used to that damned incline. Meanwhile, Peter loped towards me with ease.

'I'm glad I caught you today.'

Hope ignited within my chest.

Was it possible he remembered?

He extended a book in my direction. I stared at it.

'You lent it to me last month?'

Understanding smothered hope and I scolded myself for being so foolish. Peter either didn't notice or was too polite to draw attention to my awkwardness; I suspect it was the former. He ran his fingers through his hair in a way that used to make me swoon. Ninety years and he hadn't changed a bit.

'Anyways, I didn't get to finish but I wanted to get it back to you before . . . well . . . you know, in case my name gets called tonight and . . .'

Of course, it was always about the Draw. I tried not to scowl as I took a closer look at the book. It was an old murder mystery. I'd found it in the attic years ago, after my parents had left. It had belonged to my dad; my mum had more of a penchant for non-fiction. Either way, I'd read it so many times I knew the story by heart.

'Are you sure you don't want to keep it?' I wiped away the sweat that ran down my cheek and adjusted my groceries on my shoulder. 'I don't mind.'

Peter beamed.

'Okay. Okay! Yeah!' He shoved the book in the back pocket of his shorts, exactly the same way he had done when we were in school together. 'Thanks, Mini. You're the best. I had just gotten to the good part – a woman fell from the sky. I'll get it back to you as soon as I finish if . . . well, you know.'

Again, his fingers went to his hair. I mumbled something about not worrying and set off for home. If I hurried, I could heat up my penne al forno before having to leave again for the Draw.

*

I woke up at sunrise on the day of my party. All week, I'd sweated over the fluctuating weather forecasts. Rain, sun, partly cloudy, the weatherman couldn't seem to make up his mind. The night prior he'd predicted the return of winter. I'd fallen asleep in tears.

When the first rays of light brightened my room, I leapt out of bed and to my window. There wasn't a cloud in the sky.

'Yes! YesYesYes!' I shrieked. If my shouts didn't wake my parents, then my feet pounding across the hall and down the stairs certainly did the trick.

I burst outside in shorts and a tank top. A breeze brought goose-bumps to my skin but winter was nowhere in sight. I did cartwheels across the dew-covered grass yelling in triumph until I was covered in dirt and sweat.

My parents were sipping coffee in the kitchen when I came back in. My dad put down his mug and walked over to give me my usual birthday hug.

'Happy Birthday, Madison.' He always used my real name when addressing me.

'Da-ad.' I groaned and pulled away.

'Don't you da-ad me. I know you're growing up – too fast if you ask me – but it doesn't matter. You will always be my little girl.' He tussled my hair and I stepped back to get away.

'Happy Birthday, Mini.' My mum hugged her coffee to her chest as she eyed me from her spot at the kitchen counter. 'Now go get in the shower before you catch your death. Or worse, get the house dirty.'

I did as I was told. Nothing could ruin my perfect day.

*

I walked through the kitchen and to the fridge, to put away my ready meals. It was all the same, despite the fact my parents had left twenty years ago. As I stepped onto the small stool to pop my pasta into the microwave I could practically hear my mother from her spot at the counter.

Another TV dinner? Really, Mini? Why don't you try to cook?

I scowled at her ghost as I collected a fork and knife and laid them out next to the can of orange soda on the table. I could count the number of times she'd tried to teach me to cook over our last fifty years together. Three. Three times.

It was always after she'd caught me heating up something in the microwave. The pots and pans would emerge from the cupboards and she'd stand over me barking directions. I never did manage to do it the way she wanted and would end up evicted from the kitchen while she finished up. The one lesson I learned: only use the microwave when she wasn't around.

Beep. Beep. Beep.

I grabbed salt, pepper, onion powder, garlic granules, and shredded mozzarella and brought them to the microwave. My dad taught me this trick. Two minutes before the meal was done, add the extra seasoning and cheese, for a semi-homemade touch. He was right. They came out better every time.

I ate my dinner in silence. There was no point trying to watch TV. All the channels would be repeating the same news in preparation for tonight's event. Once I finished, I cleaned up before opening my chocolate.

Happy Birthday to me.

I unwrapped the paper sleeve, exposing the gold foil.

Happy Birthday to me.

My fingers carefully unfolded each crease.

Happy Birthday to me-e.

I broke off four squares from the bar.

Happy Birthday to me.

As the chocolate melted in my mouth, I wished I hadn't pulled away from my father's last birthday hug.

*

The day had been absolutely perfect.

A scattering of puffy, white clouds puttered against a brilliant blue sky, an extension to the bunting, cardboard palm-tree cut-outs, and balloons already decorating my party. The sun played its part, flushing our skin with its warmth. And a gentle breeze, plus regular dips into the pool, kept us in sheer, pre-summertime bliss.

Everyone I invited showed up – including Peter. The way his tan skin had glistened against those red swim trunks had warmed me more than the sun ever could. I flitted from clique to clique, the perfect hostess.

Even the last-minute, store-bought chocolate cake had been a success. When I blew out my candles, I wished every birthday could be just as magical. And as the day wrapped up, with everyone laid out on the deck, I convinced myself my wish could become reality.

*

By the time I left my house again, the sky was a canvas of red and orange. In the distance, the glint of the ocean shimmered and I trotted down the hill, past empty houses, and through abandoned streets. I was late. I'd purposefully dawdled savouring my chocolate. It was my birthday after all.

I made it to the square just as this year's mayor started talking, 'Welcome, welcome everyone.' Sandra waved her arms to quiet the crowd. In her tracksuit and ponytail, she looked more like the track and field star she was in school than our elected leader. Nevertheless, we all settled down and listened.

'First of all, I want to thank this year's events crew for their hard work getting the square ready for tonight's Draw.'

Everyone had been on that crew. When these draws first started, they'd arranged flowers, put out chairs, and shrouded the street-lights. Now, the job consisted of sweeping up any stray leaves. Still, we all clapped politely.

'As we all know, this will be my last act as mayor for the year. Depending on how the Draw goes, maybe ever.' She laughed uncomfortably at her own joke and a few people in the crowd joined in. 'Tonight, we will also redistribute jobs . . .'

'Mini.'

I turned towards my whispered name. Alice stood beside some azalea bushes. I walked over reluctantly.

'. . . if anyone hasn't put in their name for job placements, there is still time . . .'

Alice leaned close, 'So? Is your name in the Draw?'

Sandra saved me from having to answer. '. . . but we will get to the administrative tasks later. I know what we are all waiting for. Let's get on with the Draw.'

A few people clapped. Others cheered. Most of us, however, just breathed.

'Will this year's participants please step forward?'

Peter was the first onto the stage, followed quickly by Derrick, Ben, Fiona, and Fiona's mother – I couldn't believe she hadn't volunteered for stasis. Her husband had gone in with the rest of our parents and grandparents. But she just couldn't leave her daughter.

Alice glanced at me as I made my way forward. I caught the tail end of her whispered thought, '. . . knew it.'

I stood next to Fiona's mother. She had a name. I'd been repeatedly reminded of it but I couldn't seem to retain it. There was something odd about parents having names.

'I know we all are familiar with the rules but protocol . . .' Sandra shrugged apologetically and carried on. 'We will draw two names. All slips of paper are exactly the same, they've been verified by this year's teams, and each of you has your name on exactly one sheet of paper.'

I wondered if they'd put my actual name on the slip. I wondered if anyone even remembered my real name.

'Once the names have been drawn, you know the choices: jump or drink. The winners will perform their chosen action and depending on the results, we will either begin going through administrative tasks or . . . if this is finally our year . . . celebratory drinks will be on me!'

The crowd cheered. They always did.

It had been ninety years since Death died, and we were still hoping for a miracle.

*

I never got a chance to celebrate another party. By the time everyone figured out what was happening birthdays were deemed obsolete. We had stopped aging. What was the point?

Every year I wished my mum might make me another cake. My dad might give me another birthday hug. Instead, on what should have been my sixty-third birthday, they'd told me they'd signed up for stasis.

'I don't get it! Why are you guys doing this to me?'

My mum looked at my dad. I didn't understand their unspoken words.

'Dad! Dad. You can't leave me.'

My mum looked away.

'Madison.' He stepped towards me but I backed up.

'Fiona's mum is staying.' My shouts turned into a whisper. 'It's voluntary. You don't have to go into stasis. Is being around me that bad?'

My dad grabbed me by the shoulders. 'Never.' His eyes glittered. 'But Madison, it's not natural. Your mother and I should be . . . You deserve the chance to make it on your own.' He tried to smile. 'Besides, we're only going to sleep for a hundred years. Think of it like an extended nap.'

I didn't laugh.

'Madison.' He pulled me into a hug. It wasn't the same. 'Before you know it, we will be reunited. You can tell us all about the things you've done. And by then . . . you will understand . . .'

The next day, they left. Life continued. We didn't have a choice.

*

'Peter Midar.'

Peter stepped forward. Once again, his hand found its way to his hair. I couldn't help but wonder what he did with my father's book.

'Madison Campbell.'

Fiona's mother put her hand gently at my back. I looked at her, confused. Frozen at fifty-five, she was the oldest person awake. Small lines bookended her smile and streaks of silver lit up her brown hair. I envied her beauty.

'Mini?'

Fiona's mother gave me a gentle nudge and I stumbled forward. I couldn't believe it. In all my years, my name had never been called while others have had their go a couple of times. I know it was childish but it was like I was finally receiving a birthday present.

Sandra stepped up to Peter. 'Drink or Jump?'

He bit his lower lip. 'Drink?'

His answer came out more like a question and Sandra politely waited for him to confirm.

'Yes, drink.'

Someone handed her a cup from the crowd and she passed it into Peter's overly large hands. He had been fourteen when time stopped. With extremities too long for his torso, he was constantly tripping over himself. He almost knocked the cup out of Sandra's hands and blushed as she recovered it.

Of course, everyone talked but no one who had chosen 'drink' could agree on the flavour. Some said it was great – tasted like strawberry shortcake – while others said it was closer to tar. Either way, Peter raised his glass in a toast.

The crowd took in a breath of air.

He downed it in one go.

No one moved.

When Peter started coughing, we all leaned forward, anticipation burning us from within.

'Sorry.' He held up a hand. 'Sorry, it went down the wrong way.'

Everyone groaned. Sandra's nostrils flared. She took the cup away from Peter and handed it off before standing in front of me.

'Drink or Jump?'

I didn't hesitate. 'Jump.'

The crowd's interest was reengaged. The last time someone had chosen jump was directly before stasis. She'd physically been eight years old.

I turned to face the cliffs and ocean behind me. The sun was almost below the horizon and inky purple was bleeding across the sky. Down the way to the right, I saw the old, abandoned pool house.

I stepped towards the edge.

Niamh Griffin
PERIOD PAIN

There are three mugs of coffee in the kitchen. The only one that is still warm is almost empty; the remnants of Maeve's breakfast. The cafetière is full of used coffee grounds and the sink is full of dishes. You pick up the warm mug and finish it. That's all the caffeine you're allowed.

The day stretches before you. Long in the way days in late March feel. You've been afforded an extra hour and everybody seems so delighted for it, for all the chores or life they'll squeeze into its sixty minutes. You leave the messy kitchen and walk to the bathroom. Every inch of floor and wall is tiled in cold ceramic. It's sterile and the fake green plants you bought to liven it up really don't help. The grout between the tiles is yellowy in places, but in others it's stark white from where you scrapped out the dirt with a screwdriver the last time you were waiting.

You turn the knob of the shower and water bursts through, cold at first. It always takes a minute. You have a piss as you wait, checking the toilet paper before you throw it away. The water is hot now, and as you stand under the flowing stream the glass door steams up. You admire your breasts, which are swollen with hormones, and smile at the slight swell of your stomach. You like your body; the nine stones of fat, bone, tissue and whatever else that make you up. The phases of fake tan and mild eating disorders are behind you, and now you're just pale and soft and grand. 'You're absolutely grand,' you think.

You turn off the water. From the shower you can reach the back of the door and you grab your towelling dressing gown. It's damp from where Maeve must have used it this morning. You each have one, but they're matching so this often happens.

You haven't eaten yet today and spend the next few moments contemplating how you'll feed yourself. Maeve is at work. She often works weekends. Is that what has sustained your relationship through the last seven years, you wonder, as you route through your shared wardrobe for a jumper.

You do not think of how you felt when you first met her. That nauseating, dizzy feeling that encapsulated you and carried you so casually into a same-sex relationship for the first time. You don't think of sweaty nights crammed into the smoking area of The George with new, sparkly friends and rich conversations. Instead you think of Malachy and how you'd likely be pregnant by now if you'd stayed with him or with any of the other men that filled up your teens and twenties. He was lovely Malachy, with his photochromic lenses and Doc Marten shoes.

When you're dressed you take yourself into the kitchen to prepare a bowl of muesli. As you fetch the milk you see the note Maeve has attached to the fridge. *Top Secret Information*, it says, and it's folded into a perfect square and stuck with a magnet to the door. You unwrap it and inside are her bank card details and instructions to: *Book us a holiday. You choose. I pay.*

You bring your cereal outside to the small balcony that's cast off the living room. It's the first time this year you've attempted breakfast outside and there's a bite to the air that you didn't expect. A dull ache sits heavily in your lower abdominal, but as you stretch your legs out along the second patio chair it fades.

There is nothing, not a single thing, you need to do today. Maeve could point out a thousand things that need doing: a big shop, a quick hoover, a clear out, a cleanup. You can think of nothing. When you've finished eating you wander back inside. There's a wine glass on the coffee table.

Maeve got up in the middle of the night. She must have drunk it then. That means there's a bottle open in the fridge. What you wouldn't give.

You pick up the telly remote, then put it down. You pick up your phone and turn on your radio app. You listen to two ads before you turn that off too. Soon your friend Julie texts asking to meet for coffee in the Phoenix Park. You probably shouldn't, but you accept the invitation and the date is made.

Julie is already there by the time you arrive two hours later, a baby latched onto her succulent breast. Her skin's blotchy and she is wearing worn leggings. She stays seated and feeding as you get close. You act unfazed by what she's doing, but really you want to study these two creatures, stuck together like a periwinkle to a rock.

'How's it goin? You look fab,' you say, bending down to kiss her cheek.

'Ah here, the cut of me,' she says, and it's clear she doesn't care what she looks like, now she has the joys of a baby.

'Hello, would ye look at you?' you say, in the high-pitched voice you use for children. 'He's massive. God, he's grown so quick,' you tell Julie, like she doesn't know the size of her own child.

He finishes his meal, and she fixes her t-shirt and lifts him into the high chair that you've only just realised is at your table. She fusses over him until he looks happy. You wonder, are her breasts dribbling? Shouldn't she wipe them after a feed? There is so much you don't know. Where did the high chair come from? You look around the outdoor café. It's packed and understaffed. How did she manage to get this chair?

You start chatting and Julie, in fairness to her, isn't complaining about being tired or run ragged.

She keeps asking about you, saying she needs stories from the real world. You tell her you're thinking of a holiday to Italy this year. She ogles over the idea and you stare at the baby. His fat cheeks are crispy with an orange rash. He looks up at you with a wide, vacant expression and for a moment you think he's hideous, and that maybe you don't want one. But you say 'ahhh' and tilt your head to the side.

Julie is talking now about a divorcing couple she knows. Well, you both know them, but she knows them better.

'And Amanda is back on Tinder,' she said gleefully, her eyes shiny with the details of the story.

As she speaks you feel it. You're not sure at first, but then you're sure. Between your legs there is moisture forming. You focus, you concentrate. Yes, you are wet. But maybe you're horny, or maybe you've just pissed yourself a bit.

'What are you getting? I'm having a ginger tea,' Julie says. 'And fuck it, a slab of carrot cake.'

'I'll get them,' you say and you stand.

'Would you stop?' she says, and you start this little dance that you always do about paying.

You drop back to your seat and she walks away having won the dance.

The café is packed, but you don't care. Your jeans are baggy, mum-style jeans; you shove your hand beneath the waistband. You touch yourself. You're watching your surroundings. A girl, no more than fourteen, turns her head abruptly as you catch her looking. Your hand is out from your pants now, resting on your lap. You look at your fingers. They're stained in pale, red blood. It's faint. It's faint, but it's there. The baby makes distressed noises. You reach your bloodstained fingers and touch his plump arm. You squeeze it, maybe a little too tightly.

Julie is back and you take the tea and sip it. You swallow down mouthfuls of cake. You think you're doing well. You're participating in the chat, but it's not enough apparently.

'Are you all right?' she asks accusingly, like you're hiding some piece of glorious gossip from her.

'Sorry, just conscious of the time, I've yoga in the Elbow Rooms at four.'

'Jesus, I'd give my left arm for a yoga class.'

*

You've said your goodbyes and you're walking home. Your mood has lifted. Spotting can be positive, a sign of implantation, you think to yourself. You feel dry now. Your breasts aren't hurting the way they usually do this time of the month and you're definitely experiencing some nausea.

Then you're home. You turn on your radio app again. *The Parting Glass* is playing. You stand in the living room. Only your potted palm tree skews you from the view of whoever walks past. For now, this doesn't seem important. You open the button of your jeans and they fall to your ankles. You can see already that your knickers are stained in deep crimson. You take them off carefully and hold them in the cup of your hand. There is a dark, rubbery blood clot in their centre.

'Is that you? Is that you, baby Aoife?' you ask aloud. Later you'll feel foolish about this moment, but here and now it seems possible. You've read about chemical pregnancies: mini miscarriages that are mistaken for periods. You touch the clot and think how odd it feels and how strange it is that you've never touched one before. In your twenty-plus years of periods you've never thought to touch a clot. You're impressed by its solidness and its perfect, tepid temperature. You want to push it back inside you and give her another chance to cling on.

In moments you've pulled yourself together. You've hobbled to the bathroom with your thighs pressed tight. You've wiped yourself, changed your underwear and padded up. Your dirty knickers are in the laundry basket, and you're dressed in fresh clothes. You go into the kitchen and take the white wine from the fridge. The glass you pour tastes acidic. It's cheap and you don't want it, but you drink it because you can.

You open your MacBook. Your last question to Google is still displayed in its search box.

What's the length of a typical cycle?

Below is a list of websites answering your query, underneath each one it reads: *You've visited this page 7, 8, 12 times before.* You delete the question. *Cycling holidays in Italy*, you type instead and then there are loads of new pages to choose from. All fresh and never visited before. You start reading about vineyards, *al dente* pastas and travel insurance. You think of the sun on your skin and sweet, fruity wines, but you don't want to be in Italy. You burn too easily and cycling drunk in that heat sounds horrific. You take out your phone.

Period came, you type to Maeve and add a sad-faced emoji, the one with tears streaming down its yellow cheeks.

I'm sorry, honey, she writes back almost instantly, but instead of the word honey she uses an emoji of a small honey pot.

It's fine. We can try again, you reply, as if you both have big jobs that can afford to try again, as if you haven't already spent fourteen thousand euro on this, as if there's still a real chance it will work.

That evening you argue the way you often do now.

'I've six months left before I'm forty,' you yell at her. 'Then I'm done. Then I have to be done.'

She slams the bedroom door, puts on her headphones and blares music so loud she'll have hearing damage by the time she's fifty. You say you're sleeping on the couch, but by midnight you have pushed open the bedroom door and climbed in beside her.

'Just once more,' you plead softly as she curls herself around you. 'There won't always be eggs, but there'll always be Italy,' you say, almost teasingly. She doesn't reply and you notice, that from around your waist, her grip has loosened because she's tired now, you both are.

Joseph Hardy
SEWING

This new girl
is sewing my feelings
to my heels. *Tight,*
she says, *so they won't wander.*
Little stitches, little scars,
she says, piercing and pulling
to knit us together, drawing
the knot tight
to bite the thread
as my grandmother did
when she was mending.

BURNT SPOONS

All the spoons
in the drawer were burnt.
I would have bought more
if it would have kept her,
more clean spoons
for her to burn.
But they ran out
and I did
eventually too,
not wanting to see
the end.

I WISH I KNEW THEIR STORY

Very early on a Sunday in December, we found a new ball in a
park where we walk, one of those big thin-skinned balls, coated
in frost but miraculously round and pink as fresh bubblegum
nearby a tangled clump of something silver as an astronaut's suit
emerging from snow crust—I told my dog to leave.

Monday, crows stalked melting islands on the grass.
The ball, borrowed and abandoned, floated
on wood shavings near the swings. A child's quilted vest,
pristine, shiny as a juice pack, had been hung on the park rules
sign, a smaller sodden twin of it left on the ground beneath.

Tuesday, the two vests gleamed, as if waiting for sale, laid flat
and squared on a park bench. The ball, stuck beneath a far
boundary fence, had shrunken in cold. Wednesday, one vest had
been pushed onto the other for someone to sit, the ball was gone.

A. M. Havinden
SEA CHAPEL

This week; the sermon is salt
and the taste of it as song. A clean, cold burn

quickens the blood. Unseen, underfoot,
deep notes of wrack and weed wind

ankles. We raise our voices
in bright blasphemy, in shock and defiance

a hymn of human-scale endurance,
how great and small we are;

how outrageously alone; how far
we've come, suddenly, from shore.

Antonia Kearton
A BENEDICTION

There's a boulder by the forest path,
left by the ice ten thousand years ago,
it waits, patterned with lichen

the quietest blue, yellow soft as cream,
knee-high, flat-topped, so wide
I cannot wrap my arms around it –

small hands of moss patter up its side.
It's nothing like my grandmother's table
at Easter, but that's what comes to mind,

dark brown and shining under the white cloth,
bearing the feast, eggs dyed with onion skins
and at the centre, sweet pashka

a resurrection of butter, eggs, and cream,
radiant with bright sugared fruits –
moss green, rowan red, the sun's strong yellow.

Zachary Kluckman
BREAK IN CASE OF SILENCE

When fireflies dance from the open wound of your mouth.
When you have talked graves free of their bones, dug wasps
from their homes. Stung truth with a raw tooth. When grief has
bitten your hand for feeding it the names of the lost. When you
have found a secret garden within the reckless brambles of your
heart, where the silence deepens until trees wail by comparison.
When you carry fear like a corpse because the smell is more
familiar than flowers.

When the rain digs songs from the mud. When scars are rubbed
for their genies until blood appears under your nails. When your
mother takes up magic, and learns only one trick. How to open
the earth with her body and be swallowed. When your voice is a
love note written inside of a kite. An attempt to sweeten the sky.
When the string breaks. Have you seen how they dance, fireflies?

How they treat the small space inside of jars to the movement of
light. How they burn, whether their worlds shatter or not. How
the lightning must have spoken to their mothers. How their
bodies lift from the earth. How the earth fell over her body. The
grasshoppers with their bagpipes. The world with its drunken
spin. How they stop.

How you learned from your mother's tongue. The words of
passing. But also, the music of laughter. But also, the sweet scent
of grass from her lungs. Her strength. Speak them for the spring.
For the passing of light through the trees. Even if the words hang
like bruised fruit from your teeth. Even if the shadows crawl
from the ground into your arms. This is natural. This is the
wisdom of bodies. To hold what is dead close to the heart. To
break the silence with the only voice you have left.

Joshua Lander

THIS IS THE MOST BEAUTIFUL LOVE LETTER
EVER WRITTEN

It's gotta have a sick line about love. Something really deep. No roses or chocolates or anything like that. Maybe go down the Carol Ann Duffy road and whip out a vegetable? Not an onion, obviously, Duffy's got dibs on that, but something as symbolically weighty. Avoid the phallic stuff, tho. No carrots or parsnips. You don't wanna start making comparisons. Maybe a potato? Yeah, a potato – that works, because you gotta peel those layers off to get to the really good stuff . . . and then douse it in water to get rid of the starch, and that – maybe that – could be like the metaphor for her breaking it off with me, ya know? So there we go: we've got a potato on the cards and it's beautiful, right? Maybe you could say something like she's gotta bake me in her oven? Maybe not. Maybe something else. Come back to this.

Remember, you're funny. Like real, real, funny. So, make her laugh. Not at you, though. Don't, for example, tell her about the time you brought a raw egg into your viva and how it broke in your jacket and dripped onto the table which made it look like you'd come on the desk. Don't tell her that. Don't tell her about how you passed your viva but felt so incredibly depressed after you convinced yourself six months later that you hadn't really passed because it was only on a single author and your internal clearly hated the project so much you know in your heart of hearts it wasn't actually a real pass and you don't deserve to have a PhD. Don't tell her any of that. Talk about how you're an *academic* now. A Doctor. Doctor Silverman, PhD in Literature, Theology, and the Arts. That sounds good. That sounds powerful and impressive. Never mind the abandoned book. Never mind the failed career in academia. You don't need to talk about that. Tell her a joke. Keep it light and casual and breezy. Extra, extra, breezy.

The key thing here is to be cool. Coolness is how you win her affection. You were cool when you met her. Remember when you met her? God, you were happy. For years, you had thrush coming out your ass: red, raw, itchy thrush and then one day you went and got happy and POOOOF – it disappeared. And you were walking thrush-free like a normal person. You were swaggering happily along without having to stick a sneaky finger up your bum to settle the scratch down. You walked for hours and hours, showboating your bum's ability to not burst into flames. Then you and her matched on Tinder and you were really clever and cool and funny because you could walk for hours without scratching your bum; you felt confident and capable and when she asked you, super casual like, if you wanted to go back to hers, you did so nonchalantly, as though you weren't at all fazed that this woman was asking you back to her place, even though you and her both knew what that meant: sex – holy fucking shitballs, S–E–X. And best of all, because your asshole wasn't itchy and sore and red you went and had good sex; it wasn't like the mind-blowing sex you would go on to have later, because, well, let's not get carried away here, but it was *good* with an emphasis on the ooooooo. Remember that when you write this letter; it's key to show her that you've still got it. You're still that guy. You can still have sex. You don't cry after masturbating. Fuck no, that's not you. That's not your style. You're still the guy from way back when. So make sure to tell her all that.

But don't make it nostalgic. You're not doing this because you are hankering for the days of yore or anything like that. You're all about being present. You're into mindfulness, these days. You're Captain Chill. You smoke weed now. You even buy your own stuff and have your own dealer. You meditate and do yoga. You're the new and improved You. Sure, you've started eating meat again, but don't tell her that. Just pretend you don't, and we'll deal with it after. Maybe tell her you're going to be a teacher now. Will she like that? Maybe . . . Teachers are kind of straight-laced and dull, though. Maybe tell her you're only gonna be a teacher until you get that book deal. That it's just a means to an end. You're gonna be a writer. She'll fucking love that. Who doesn't love a writer? Especially a writer like you. Tell her about the novel you're working on. Be sure to mention it's on the Holocaust. She'll be impressed by that. She'll like that you're exploring your history. She'll think you're deep and serious and stuff.

Be poetic, too. But don't be clichéd. You don't just read Mary Oliver anymore. Sure, by all means, mention her casually. She's her favourite poet, so it's worth slipping her into the conversation. But be really subtle about it. You don't continuously listen to readings of 'Wild Geese' and 'The Journey' and cry in the shower. No, of course not. Nor, whilst we're on the subject of crying, do you still watch the birthday video she made for you on YouTube. Those Russian bots, I reckon, are responsible for all those views. You read other poets now. Make sure to name a Black poet or two. She'll be impressed by how woke you are. But don't, for fuck sakes, say you're woke. Nobody woke ever calls themselves woke; that would make them virtue signallers, tokenistic gesturers. You know, phoneys. And you're not a phoney. You're real and serious. Deadly serious. Tell her when you get a salary you're gonna donate money to BLM. Maybe to Palestine, too. Maybe both, you haven't decided. Tell her how hard it is to think about what charities deserve your money most. She'll recognise how charitable you are, and she'll remember how concerned and caring you have always been.

Maybe don't tell her you listen to Bukowski after every wank. That's a bit weird, that. Do other men listen to poetry after they've masturbated? I hope so. Maybe ask the therapist. Oh, remind her that you see a therapist. She'll remember how reflective you are. You're always willing to have a big old chat about your feelings because you're always doing that anyway. You're a writer, after all, and a writer is all about expression and feeling. You've got a beautiful inside, especially now that the thrush has cleared up.

What else? Nature. She fucking loved nature. She loved the trees and the leaves and the branches and the birds and all that stuff. So make sure to mention that. Tell her how you listen to the sound of the wind and stand and stare at the petals of the flowers. Maybe mention how you have thought about posting flowers on Instagram but chickened out because you didn't want to seem contrived. Tell her that you love being outdoors because of how pure it all is. You feel all peaceful and serene when you're around the sea. You love watching birds fly, even pigeons, and you adore the sound of the seagulls squawking in the early hours of the morning. God, she'll read this, and she'll remember: she'll remember how layered you are. Like an onion, amirite, Carol?

Don't forget to mention your spiritual turn. I mean it's all well and good being an atheist because organised religion is so obviously corrupt and wicked – definitely use 'wicked' here – but you've come to realise, after spending so much time outside of the city, that there's something real here in the world, and the only word you can muster for it is *spiritual*. And you don't know exactly what it means, and she'll think that's fantastic, too, because precision isn't sexy. Factuality isn't what anyone wants. No, it's gushing, vivacious pontification! You, the eternal philosopher, are always lost in thought, running around with yet another idea regarding the meaning of life, a theorem that is beyond any words or formulas. It can't be explained, because words inevitably fail your extraordinary ideas.

Tell her all that. Remind her of just how beautiful a mind you have. Who could possibly resist such an extraordinary letter? It's perfect. She'll read this and realise what a huge, huge mistake she's made. She'll call you straight away. No WhatsApp or Facebook. Straight on the phone. *I'm sorry*, she'll cry, *I never knew! I never knew!* And you'll be so chill about it. You'll slowly rise up off the bench press, where you've just finished yet another PR, and you'll tell her it's okay, you still love her, and you're ready to try again. And she'll be so grateful. And you'll move out there to be with her. And you'll both live happily ever after. Just as soon as she reads this and realises: This is the Most Beautiful Love Letter Ever Written.

Juliet Lovering
KINDLING

I felt I was in the way but that I shouldn't leave. My father had already left. His empty cup was in the sink and there was a dusting of dry mud by the door where his boots had been. My mother was leaning on her elbows over the kitchen table, swaying from side to side. She was making a sound like a 'whuu' over and over. It started off breathy and light but changed to a low groan that seemed to come from deep in her belly. It would be another hour before a grey dawn broke.

From the kitchen window, I watched the smoke emerging at an angle from the tallest chimney in the street behind and wondered whether it was the tail end of last night's fire or the meagre beginnings of the morning's. To feel useful, I washed out my father's cup and swept the dust from the floor. I got my mother a glass of water and left it beside her on the table.

The cold crept down my neck and in at the cuffs of my dressing gown and it made my skin hurt. With my coat on over the top, I went outside to fill the coal scuttle from the bunker by the back door. The frost crunched beneath my feet and my breath plumed and froze before me. The rasp of the shovel startled the pigeons and sent them thrumming into the air, wings pulsing. Worried my mother would complain about the cold air rushing in, I shut the door behind me with my shoulder. She didn't flinch. The weight of the scuttle made me walk with a waddle all the way through to the sitting room. I kept my coat on while I raked over the remains of fire from the night before, clearing the ash and saving the small rocks of coal that could be used again. My hands were clumsy from the chill and the front piece slipped from my fingers, making a heavy clunk on the tiles. As the mess from the ash pan slid into the metal caddy, clouds of dust puffed up around the room, suspended for a moment, before the draw of the chimney sucked the greater part back up and out. It would be my job to clean the ornaments on the mantlepiece once the residual dust settled. Taking individual sheets from the pile of old newspapers, I folded concertinaed blocks, enough to fill the grate, and laid the kindling over the top. I had a silly fear of matches and of burning my fingers and wasted several, striking them and dropping them in too quickly before the flame could take hold.

With the slow scuff of the leather soles of her slippers on the rug, my mother made her way through to the sitting room. She straightened up briefly in the doorway, supporting her back with her hands and took a few easy breaths. The flames had taken hold and the kindling was crackling. 'You'll need to get the others to school,' she said, bending over again, 'and then get the nurse.' By then I felt sure I knew what was going to happen, but I had little idea how. I took out a few choice coals from the scuttle using the bird-foot tongs that had been my grandmother's, and which I'd always found pleasingly grotesque, and laid them carefully, one by one, over the kindling.

Our school uniforms hung over the banisters, two pairs of trousers and three dresses. I took the others' vests and pants and put them inside my dressing gown to warm them up. The thought of getting out from under the warmth of the covers made school mornings a struggle and there was a knack to the transition. I woke them gently and checked their feet. If they were bare, I felt around under the blankets for the woolly bed socks that had worked their way off during the night.

Once everyone had their clothes on and had thundered downstairs to the kitchen the whole house seemed properly awake. A clipped Home Counties voice from the wireless brought the news from the BBC in London. It seemed remote, almost ridiculous. James and David stuck their noses in the air and, in a superior tone, recounted village trivialities with great seriousness.

'Bannerman's are currently able to offer their customers a jolly good deal on mince,' said David.

'Mr Lawson has begun work on a fortified fence to protect next season's dahlias from local reprobates,' said James.

'Beattie's is selling oxter-ticklers, three for the price of two. Mrs Morris is said to be delighted by this development,' said David. Lizzy sat upright, turned to Margaret and opened her mouth to speak but collapsed into giggles before she could share the joke.

At the school gates, James promised to tell the teacher what I was doing. I crossed the main road and ran down the hill towards the bay, watching my breath before me. The sky was overcast and it was difficult to identify the horizon. A low mist hung over the houses and the kirkyard and its heavy iron gate was wedged open with a large stone. The rhythm of the waves, heavy and powerful, always suggested a sort of enduring force. Listening to them was comforting, but I understood their threat.

The nurse's house was at the bottom of the hill, sideways on to the sea and the steep shingle beach. I knocked hard and then pulled down at the sleeves of my coat to cover my hands. She rummaged around inside for a few moments before opening the door, cape and hat already on. She nodded and gestured with a flick of her finger that I should make my way quickly back to school.

At lunchtime, I ran home but slowed down when I heard the howling from several doors away. I slipped in quietly and went straight through to the kitchen for a slice of bread and butter and a glass of milk. When the crying had died down, I poked my head round the door and saw my mother lying exhausted on the bed. She looked like she'd been dragged out of the sea, an empty wasted creature out of place, her body behaving differently now that it was on land and unsupported by water. Her hair was soaked through with perspiration and her eyes were glassy and unfocused. In an enamel kidney dish at the foot of the bed, a fresh white terry nappy had been stitched shut. I had such a strange feeling. The air was different; it wasn't cold anymore. Something had disappeared and something else was there suspended in the ether.

The nurse put her pen and papers down and, putting her arm around me, ushered me out the room. 'Can you fetch your Auntie Anne?' she asked. I didn't like my aunt's house. It was sparsely furnished and the furniture she did have was stained a nasty dark brown. It seemed designed for discomfort. Above the doorframe in the hallway was a faded cross-stitch on a discoloured Aida background which read 'God is the strength of my heart and my portion forever'. The idea of a portion, when portions were fiercely contested in our house, brought to my mind a rather parsimonious God, but certainly the one of my aunt's imagination. She looked perpetually inconvenienced and her lips seemed always to turn downwards at the edge. In this instance, she seemed cheered to have a witness to her inconvenience, and she made a performance of getting her bag, her knitting and her coat.

From a street away we could hear the piercing cry. It was so intrusive, so deeply unpleasant it made me angry. I would have done anything to make it stop. I must have slowed down, and my aunt, sensing this, and with unusual warmth, placed her hand in the small of my back. Without applying any pressure, she made it clear I was to keep going. But I couldn't make myself go back in. I bucked and ran, shouting behind me that I'd be back after.

She was still there when school had finished for the day. She wasn't cross with me, as I'd feared. Instead, she sat with my mother in the bedroom, only occasionally coming down to whisper at us to keep the noise down, and then at tea-time, to ladle out soup and butter bread. My father didn't come home for dinner and still wasn't back when I got into bed. I wondered if he'd heard the crying too. I woke with a fright at the sound of the empty milk bottles clattering on the pavement. The front door was usually left open but my aunt, particular about these things, had locked it. My bed was pushed up against the gable end and I heard the back gate open and smash against it. A walk of few seconds took a great deal longer as my father lurched and staggered bumping into each wall, one smooth and harmless, the other harled and abrasive.

He swore a number of times before making it in the back door and onto the sofa.

*

We were all dressed in our best clothes. At the bottom of the stairs, my mother reached out to hug me, but winced as she pulled my head to her chest. She had a sour metallic smell and I didn't want to be near her. Her body seemed a different kind of thing. She put her arm around me and together we looked into the little sitting room, which was still bitterly cold. The small silver box was on the central panel of the barley twist table. 'I'll take her,' my father said. He walked out into the middle of the road with the silver box under his arm. Uncle Alec and Uncle Mo stood on either side of him. We all filed out behind them and Auntie Anne helped Mum down the single step, guiding her by the arm. She ushered her around the patch of ice that had formed underneath a hole in the guttering. When it rained the water dripped and froze into an almost invisible hazard. Mo nodded and they started to walk towards the church. People stopped on the pavement and stood, heads lowered, until we were past. The wind blew from the north carrying the peculiar smell from the smokeries in the next village, a smell that was often closer to lilies than burnt wood and fish. My father let out a high-pitched gasp. In a kind of reflex action, Uncle Alec slapped him hard on the back as if the noise and force would sort him out.

*

The fire was out and the sitting room was bone cold. I raked the coals and let the ash fall through. Lizzy came in and picked up the tongs, laughing as she made them open and shut and walk along the hearth like an absurd half-bird. 'Can I help?' she asked, kneeling down beside me. I showed her how to empty the ash into the can, holding it as close to the chimney as possible. I explained the draw of the cold air from above, and how to fold briquettes from the old newspapers. We set them neatly in the grate. She opened the copper kettle to find the box of matches and sounded out the words 'Scottish Bluebell' with satisfaction. 'Do you want to light it?' I asked. She bit her lip before deciding that, yes, she did. 'You hold the box in your left hand,' I said, 'and strike the match with your right, away from you'. She was too timid to begin with and nothing happened. She tried again and again, and on the fifth go the match lit. Her face registered her delight, terror and sorrow as she flung the match too hastily onto the paper and saw the small flame extinguish.

Crìsdean MacIlleBhàin
MO SHEARMON (III)

Mo shearmon a tha cho annasach nua-fhasanta
    's gum bi èiginn air a' Ghàidhlig
    a cuarain as cliste 's as luaithe thoirt a-mach
    is ruith gu bras air a ceann dìreach 'na mo dhèidh,
    a dh'fhaicinn dè tha dol a thachairt,
    dè tha dol a dh'fhàs aiste
    agus modh-obrach cho mùiteach sgaogach agam
    nach ro-aithnichear càil, tha gach
    earalas no ro-aithris gun stàth,
    thig maoim air a' chànan bhochd seo!
Mo shearmon mar an nighean a chunnaic mi air an tram'
      a-raoir
    a bha a' dèiligeadh ri fòn-làimhe
    air dòigh cho nàdarra, neo-liobasta – theireadh tu
    gun do dh'fhàs e 'na roinn de bodhaig fhèin,
    mar a h-uileann no a cuisteag –
    air neo mar an fhàinne bhoillsgeach
    a bha crochadh bho bhun a sròine –
    ach san dol-a-mach seo, ris an fhìrinn innse,
    cha robh fàinne idir ann, is i
    'na nighinn shnasmhoir riamhaich, a' bruidhinn
    's a' bruidhinn gun sheasachas no sòradh –
    bha mis' a' fèorachadh dhìom fhìn
    nach robh math dh'fhaoidte cùrsa-feasgair ann
    far am b' urrainn do dhuine cumanta mar mise
    ionnsachadh a bhruidhinn air an dòigh sin –
    bhitheadh na h-oileanaich a' dèanamh eacarsaichean
    's iad ri còmhradh airson dà mhionaid, còig mionaidean,
    deich mionaidean gun stad – cha bhiodh e ceadaichte
    amaideas a ràdh, dh'fheumadh ciall
    is stàth bhith aig do sheantansan,

a bharrachd air sin, bhiodh tu ag ionnsachadh
mar nach toirear aire sam bith don t-saoghal mun cuairt
's tu dol air adhart a' bruidhinn le cuideigin
nach fhaicear leat a thuar no a shùilean,
aig amannan gun chluinntinn
ach sprùilleach briste dhe na thathar ag innse dhut –
ach chan fhaod thu sgur dheth,
feumaidh tu a' cheàrd gu lèir a thoirt gu buil
gun dìochuimhneachadh càit' am bu chòir dhut
teàrnadh às an tram, air neo bidh thu a' tilleadh
gu fèin-fhios ann an ceàrn dhen bhaile nach aithne dhut,
far nach tug thu aon cheum 'na do bheatha
is feumaidh tu streap suas air tram' eile
anns an t-seòladh mu choinneamh –
ach cha robh càil sam bith a' cur dragh air an nighinn ud,
's i a' dol air adhart a' bruidhinn gu sàmhach, sàsaichte
Mo shearmon aig nach eil moraltachd no oileanachd idir
gun sanas ann air cràbhachd no teagasg,
nach eil a' faighinn taice bho aon chaibidil
no teacsa goirid dhen Bhìoball, a dh'imicheas
gu cunbhalach air a dhà chois fhèin
gun chead a shireadh bho neach san t-saoghal
gun fhireanachadh no mathadh fhaighinn
bho chogais no bho chreideamh aithnichte
Mo shearmon mar bhoireannach a thèid a-steach gu seòmar
far a bheil mòran daoine 'nan cadal,
dà sheòmar a th' ann, bhon as e sgoil-shamhraidh seo
far am bi na h-òigeir, na h-òighean
's na deugairean a' cluich 's ag ionnsachadh
a bhith cluich air innealan-ciùil a dh'iomadh seòrsa –
cuirear na fireannaich is na boireannaich
a chadal an dà sheòmar air leth –

fosglaidh i na còmhlachan-uinneige mòra fiodha
a bha a' cumail a-mach an leòis
gus a' chuideachd a dhùsgadh
beag is beag, gun mhaoim gun chlisgeadh,
cha bhi ach fuaim a ceumannan sèimh'
agus leus an latha a' drùidheadh a-steach
tro na lòsaidhean gam buaireadh
– cha b' ionnan ise 's am boireannach meadhan-aosta
's mi fhìn 'nam dheugair aig fèis dhen t-seòrsa cheart
ann am Bayreuth sa Ghearmailt
rachadh sìos is suas trannsa na sgoil
san robh sinn uile fo aoigheachd
feuchainn an dèanadh i cinnteach
nach biodh sùgradh no mànran air a thoirt gu buil
leis na h-òigearan 's na h-òighean fad na h-oidhche –
dh'fhairtlich a h-oidhirp oirre,
faodaidh sibh a bhith gam chreidsinn! –
bhon as e deugairean a th' anns
a' chuid as motha dhiubh, gabhaidh iad
an ùine a bhith fosgladh an sùilean
no sìneadh a-mach an gàirdeanan –
mothaichidh am boireannach do leabaidh no dhà
is dà cholainn 'nan laighe ann, cha bhi e
'na chùis dheifreach no chudromach dhi
nochdadh an e fireannach a tha 'na laighe
còmhla ri boireannach, no dithis fhireannach,
no dithis bhoireannach ri taobh a chèile
bhon a tha ise cuideachd mothachail
do bhòidhichead nan òigear, do shùbailteachd
am buill, do neart an leisean is an calpannan –
's ann mar is' a tha mi
's mi dùsgadh cuid nach beag

dhe na faclan a ghabhas pàirt 'nam shearmon
bho na faclairean san robh iad 'nan cadal
chionn fhada, chan eil iad aosta,
is e deugairean a th' annta,
aig a bheil an cadal 'na sheòrsa ghiomnastachd
a chuireas iad gu feum a bhith
cinntinn nas luaithe fhathast,
agus nuair a dhèireas iad
às an leapannan aig a' cheann thall
bidh iad mì-fhoighidneach a thaobh
saoghal nan inbheach
le a dhòighean baoth seann-fhasanta,
fadachd aca ri gach rud
atharrachadh is tòiseachadh às ùr
Mo shearmon nach bi a' còrdadh ri fear-deasachadh
iris, ràitheachain no co-chruinneachaidh bhliadhnail
chan e a-mhàin a chionn 's gu bheil e
cho fada sìnt' a-mach, ach a chionn
's gum bruidhnear ro thric ann
mu dheidhinn feise 's feòlmhorachd –
"Tha gnothaichean ann", bidh iad ag ràdh,
"a bhios a h-uile duine dèiligeadh riutha
ann am mòmaid shònraichte dhen latha,
no dhen t-seachdain, no dhen bhliadhna,
no aon uair a h-uile dhà no trì bliadhnaichean,
no gach còig bliadhnaichean a thèid seachad –
chan e an tricead as cudromach –
ach dè am feum a th' ann a bhith tilleadh
air ais uair 's a rithist gus a' chuspair seo
is na h-uiread a ghnothaichean ann
a b' fheàrr do dhàn fada beantainn riutha?" –
bidh cuid eile fo dhragh, math dh'fhaoidte

's iad a' smaoineachadh gum bi amharas
aig leughadairean cuideigin as aithne dhaibh
a bhith falaichte fo sgàil pearsachan mo dhàn –
"Am bòcan, mar eisimpleir!"
bidh iad a' feòrachadh dhìom,
"an creutair mì-dhealbhte ud a ghabhas
àite a' mhinisteir airson sealan,
cò air a tha thu 'g amas leis a' bhòcan?
Chan eil sinn airson seasamh fa chomhair
breitheimh ann an cùirt-cheartais,
air neo bhith air ar pàighneachadh
'son dò-bheart dhen t-seòrsa sin!"
Uime seo, cha bhi e nochdadh, an dàn
a tha mi sgrìobhadh, ach mar earrannan sgapte,
mar chriomagan air an tarraing a-mach dheth
's am figheadh le chèile às ùr –
bidh mi toilichte gu lèor ma thachras sin
chionn 's nach bi coltas soilleir, socraichte
aig mo dhàn gu ceann an t-saoghail,
's e ath-nuadhaichte gun stad
mar an uilebheist san sgeulachd
a chinn ceann ùr air a h-amhaich
cho luath 's a dhèanadh slaoightear
am fear a bh' ann roimhe a sgathadh –
bithidh na daoin' a' sìor-dheasbad
ciod e 'n àireamh cheart a dh'earrannan
a mhiannaich an t-ùghdar a bhith ann
is ciod an t-sreath-leanmhainn phongail
sam bu chòir dhaibh a bhith nochdadh
Mo shearmon mar òraid àrd-ollaimh aost'
a tha air fàs sgìth dhe dhreuchd, 's e air na rudan
ceudna ràdh, na breithneachaidhean 's luachaidhean

ceudna gan ath-aithris ri ginealach
às dèidh ginealaich a dh'oileanaich
bhochda shàraichte, 's nighean no fiùran
'nan suidhe air a bheulaibh an-diugh a tha
's docha 'nan oghaichean aig cuideigin a bha
sa chiad chlas riamh a bha ag èisteachd ris,
tha na duilleagan sgrìobht' an litreachan beaga annasach
air an deasga fa chomhair buidh' is lorcach,
's iongantach a' bhragadaich a chluinnear
's e cur tè dhiubh sìos, a' gabhail 'na làimh
tè eile, an leasan cho tàmhach dùr
's gu bheil an cadal a' tighinn ort,
thu a' toirt taic dha d' cheann
le bas do làimh', cha bhi an suidheachadh
ach a' fàs nas miosa, an uair sin
bidh bruadar mìorbhaileach a' teàrnadh thugad
nas neo-chreidsinnich' ioma-fhillte eadhon
na 'm fear a bh' agad a-raoir 's an aon àrd-ollaimh
a' toirt òraid, dranndan cofhurtail
mar a thig bho sheilleanan a' tighinn
às a bheul – bliadhnaichean às a dhèidh,
is do chlann fhèin agad, an cadal air tèarnadh
mu dheireadh thall air leanabh a bha
trioblaideach is frionasach air dòigh shònraichte,
saoilidh tu gu bheil thu a' toirt buidheachais
don phroifeasar ud, chan ann a thaobh
a theagaisg no a bheachdan, ach air sgàth
nan aislingean prìseil luachmhor a theirinn thugad
nuair a bha an cadal air do bhuannachd
leis cho ràsanach dòrainneach 's a bha a shearmon.

Christopher Whyte
THE WAY I TALK (III)

The way I talk, so strange and innovative
    Gaelic will have to look out the fastest,
    most agile sandals it has and start
    scampering after helterskelter
    to find out what is going to happen,
    what is going to become of it
    seeing I go about things in such a
    volatile and inconsistent way
    it's impossible to predict anything in advance,
    forecasts and precautions have no meaning –
    this poor language is going to enter into panic!
The way I talk, like the girl on the tram yesterday
    handling her mobile phone so skilfully
    and naturally you'd say it had
    turned into a part of her own body
    like her elbow or her little finger –
    or like the gleaming ring
    hanging out of the end of her nose –
    though in this case, to tell the truth,
    there wasn't any ring at all – she was
    neatly turned out and attractive, talking
    on and on without any truce or hesitation –.
    it made me think how good it would be
    if you could sign up for an evening class
    where an ordinary person like me
    could learn how to talk the way she did –
    the students would do exercises where they
    had to speak for two, or five, or ten
    minutes without stopping – you wouldn't be
    allowed to talk nonsense, your sentences
    would have to possess meaning and content –

besides which, they would learn how
not to pay the slightest bit of attention
to the people around them, but continue
talking to someone whose face and eyes
they couldn't see, sometimes even without
hearing more than scattered bits and pieces
of what they were saying, but
you wouldn't be allowed to break off,
you'd have to bring the whole business to a conclusion
without forgetting which tram stop
you were supposed to be getting off at,
otherwise you'd risk coming to your senses
in an unknown part of the city
you hadn't set foot in at any point in your life
and be forced to get on a different tram
travelling in the opposite direction –
but nothing could deter that girl, she just
kept on talking, satisfied and contented
The way I talk, devoid of morals or edification,
with not a trace of religion or didactics,
not seeking any support from a chapter
or short text in the Bible, proceeding
steadily on its own two feet without
looking for permission from anyone in the world,
not seeking justification or pardon
from any known conscience or creed
The way I talk, like a woman entering
a room where many people are asleep,
two rooms in fact, because this is a summer school
where young men and women and teenagers
play and learn to play on
all sorts of musical instruments –

males and females go to sleep
in two separate dormitories –
she opens the big wooden shutters
that were keeping the light out
so as to wake them all up gradually
without any shock or alarm,
nothing to disturb them other than the sound
of her gentle steps and the daylight
penetrating inside through the window panes –
quite different from the middle-aged woman
when I attended a similar course as a teenager
in Bayreuth in Germany, who used to
march up and down the corridors of
the school where we were all accommodated
trying to make sure no courting or lovemaking
was going on during the night –
and you can take my word for it she didn't succeed! –
since most of them are teenagers, they take
their time opening their eyes
or stretching out their arms –
the woman notices a bed or two
with two bodies in it, but it doesn't
strike her as urgent or important
to check whether a man is lying
next to a girl, or two men together,
or two women, she is occupied observing
how lovely the young people are,
how supple their limbs, how strong
their thighs and calves – just like her,
I awaken a significant proportion
of the words in my poem out of dictionaries
in which they slept, they are not old,

more like teenagers for whom sleep
is a species of gymnastics they make use of
in order to grow faster still,
and when finally they get up
out of their beds they lose patience
with the world of adults and their stupid
old-fashioned ways, keen to change
everything and start over again
The way I talk which no editor of a magazine,
    quarterly or annual anthology is going to like,
    not just because it goes on for such a long time
    but because it touches too often
    on topics like sex and the pleasures of the flesh –
    'Certain things exist,' they will say
    'which every person has to deal with
    at a particular stage of the day,
    or the week, or the year,
    or once every two, or three, or five
    years that pass by – how often
    they do it isn't what matters – what
    need is there to keep coming back
    again and again to that one subject
    when there are so many others around
    far more appropriate for an extended poem?' –
    others perhaps will worry readers may
    suspect somebody they know lies hidden
    behind the characters in my poem –
    'Now take the goblin, for example!'
    they will ask, 'that ill-shaped creature
    who steals the minister's place for a while,
    who were you trying to get at with the goblin?
    We wouldn't want to find ourselves sitting

in front of the judge in a courtroom
and end up paying a fine for a prank like that!'
Which explains why what I'm writing
can only be published as selected fragments,
passages excerpted and woven together afresh –
I'd be perfectly happy for that to happen
because it means that till the end of the world
my poem can never have a clear and fixed form,
it will constantly get revised, like
the monster in the story that grows
a new head on its neck as soon as
some scoundrel has cut the previous one off –
there will be unending discussions
about how many sections the author
intended there to be, and what precisely
is the correct order they ought to appear in
The way I talk, like an aged professor
who has grown tired of his job
and has been saying the same things,
repeating the same judgements and evaluations
over and over to generation after generation
of poor, fatigued students, the girls
and youths sitting in front of him today
could be the grandchildren of somebody
from the first class that ever listened to him,
the pages in front of him written in
a peculiar miniature hand, yellow and tattered,
produce an amazing crackling when he
puts one down and lifts another up,
the lesson so dull and soporific
that sleep overcomes the students, you rest
your head on the palm of your hand but

that only makes things worse and then
a marvellous dream descends upon you
even more incredible and involved
than the one you had yesterday, when the same
professor was giving a lecture, a comforting
buzzing like bees emerging from his mouth –
years afterwards, when you have children of your own
and finally a child that was unbelievably
restless and fretful has fallen asleep
you will reflect that you are grateful
to that professor, not for his lessons or his opinions,
but for the glorious, exceptional dreams
that arrived when sleep overcame you
as the way he talked was so excruciatingly tedious.

English version by Shuggie McCall

D. B. MacInnes
THE SAWMILLERS

For years I ran the images in my head like some flickering newsreel. Daddo watching his hand spinning away in apparent slow motion and the yells of the other men sounding far off as if from the forest, although one of them must have hit the power button so the huge circular saw began its last few revolutions, the whirling steel now streaked with blood.

Nana was a good storyteller. She didn't skimp on the details of what led up to the accident. All that morning, the trees felled the previous day were hitched up by Daddo and his men to the two Clydesdales who then hauled them from the forest. The big saw on its conveyer belt paid no respect to the massive trunks, ripping through the heartwood as easily as the bark and sap, slicing them into planks to be hoisted onto the tall stacks growing beside the cutting shed. But then, as the final plank fell away on the last of the trunks, the saw came to an abrupt halt, snagged by a stray branch which stubbornly refused to snap.

Daddo always said it didn't seem worth a thought, to lean over the conveyer belt and twitch the offending branch away. But the laws of physics are implacable. The saw was still on full power and held the branch in its teeth at an angle. On release it was propelled away from him, taking the hand that gripped it across the saw's path.

When he came to his senses in the back of the car driven by one of the men, Nana was beside him, twisting a rod through the tourniquet with one hand and with the other feeding him whisky. He must have understood the consequences straight away. A one-handed sawmilling contractor was not going to inspire confidence amongst the forest-owning gentry, and the hiring of an extra man in the cutting shed would cripple his profit.

It was Daddo's right hand. I know this because I used to watch him changing gear with his left, the stump with the steel hook resting on the steering wheel of the Austin A40 during the long road trips we took visiting relatives across the land; a hill farmer in Angus, a shepherd and his wife in Perthshire. He and Nana would break the journey at favoured inns, leaving Ross and me in the back seat with crisps and pop while they took a dram within. Although Ross was barely one year older than me, he got the first choice of crisp flavours because, as he often reminded me, he was my uncle.

I didn't meet my grandparents and Ross until I was eight years old because of some gap, some rift in our relationship with them. The forest where they had contracted to cut timber was on the Inveraray Castle lands in Argyll. They arrived just after the war, in the lorries carrying their prefabricated cabins and saw gear. My Nana loved their itinerant life, and I can see her in the front lorry sitting beside Daddo, her eyes glittering with excitement.

The sawmill was a half-day's bus ride from Glasgow, where I lived with my mother. She had the sharp looks of the dark Celts and was a lover of parties and smart clothes. We were like flatmates, she and I, and I liked that she didn't mind sharing her library books. My father preferred army life and overseas postings to confinement with our little family in a tenement flat. The kitchen with its black coal-fired range also had an alcove with a small bed, where I lay and looked at the window which framed the stars in the night sky. Shining, immutable, steadfast, they were a kind of comfort on nights my mother didn't come home.

On these nights I trained myself to sleep with one hand over my heart and one over my mouth. I reasoned that if an intruder tried to stab me, the prick of the knife on my hand would give me warning. Equally, anyone trying to drop poison into my mouth would have to pull my other hand away first. I've always been good in the morning since then, greeting its potential with the eagerness of a survivor, and that impulse forward from hurt or doubt has remained my stratagem in life. But even now, an old man, I awake in the night with my fingers against my lips.

I spent my school holidays at the sawmill. My mother would press five shillings in the hand of the bus driver to ensure my safe delivery to Inveraray town square a few miles from my grandparents' cabin in the forest. I thought myself to be an intrepid traveller and considered the money wasted.

Nana usually met me at the terminus. As the bus came to a halt, I would look in the crowd on the pavement for her feathered hat and below it her smiling face. She loved poetry written in broad Scots, my Nana, and loved to recite it. The first time I climbed down from the bus she crouched and hugged me and then, sitting back on her heels she declared,

> There's a road to a far-aff land, an' the land is yonder
>   Whaur a' men's hopes are set;
> We dinna ken foo lang we maun hae to wander,
>   But we'll a' win to it yet.[1]

The only reason I remember this is because I have it in her handwriting, framed above my desk, on a card sent to me when she knew I would never see her again.

The sawmill and the cabins in which my grandparents and their workers lived, lay in a curl of the broad river which we listened to in our beds, the currents brawling with the rocks in their path as they rushed to complete the last few miles to the sea. It's been half a century, but if I close my eyes I can still hear that river, and smell the sharpness of newly milled timber, the woodsmoke from the stove, and Daddo's sour sweat as he entered the lean-to kitchen tacked on to the cabin. The first time I met him, Daddo lifted my hand with his hook, inspected it and said, 'Play the piano, do ye?'

Later on I secretly studied Ross's hands. He was already doing unskilled work around the sawmill and they were chapped, brown with ingrained dirt and exposure to the weather.

---

1   Violet Jacob, 'Craigo Woods' (1915)

The main room in the cabin had a stove in one corner. Packed with timber offcuts, it glowed red-hot behind the steel guard. The bedroom doors were at each end of the room. On one wall hung the galvanised tin bath we used once a week. Ross and I played Cowboys and Indians around and on top of the timber stacks by day. At night we listened to Marty Robbins' 'Gunfighter Ballads' on the wind-up gramophone, our real leather cowboy holsters and cap-guns hanging at the end of the bed.

Sometimes there were parties, a couple of people from the town, some folk from the other cabins. I remember a pair of young girls two-stepping to some accordion dance band from the radio, the stove lighting up the smiling faces around the room, as a bottle of whisky was passed from hand to hand. Always, the night finished with Daddo marching up and down, a broom doubling as a rifle held over his shoulder by his stumpy arm and hook, and he singing,

> Behold, I am a soldier bold, I'm only twenty-five
>   years old,
> A finer warrior ne'er was seen from Inverness to
>   Gretna Green.[2]

The cabins were primitive. Water from the river, heat from the stove and light from paraffin took care of the main needs. Against these disadvantages the transistor radio was a beacon of modernity. Outside there was a privy built over a pit. Behind the privy door there was a seat with a lid, a pile of old newspapers and a bucket of sawdust to throw down the hole. There was something else in there too, a thing of wonder, but perhaps it was only a trick of light that one time, because no one else ever mentioned it.

I had woken up early one winter's morning with an urgent need. I looked out of the window at the snow on the ground and could see frost glinting on the grey boards of the privy. In my duffle coat

2   Alexander Crawford, 'Jock McGraw of the Forty-twa' (1877)

and wellies, I noticed the porch door was already unlatched, but gave it no thought.

As I sat in the privy, which was so dark I had to feel for the newspaper, the early morning sun must have hit the boarding outside. A needle of light stabbed through a tiny pinhole in the larch and illuminated the wall opposite with an inverted scene. I could see the cabins and the track which wound through them towards the hazy outlines of the sawmill and timber stacks. Too young to understand the science of the camera obscura effect, it seemed to me I was witnessing a miracle, for at that time I still believed in God.

Then I heard a lorry coming up the track. I turned my head upside down, trying to see more clearly. The lorry was pulling a load of milled timber. It stopped opposite our cabin and Daddo jumped out. Some words were exchanged and then a hand appeared from the lorry window holding a roll of banknotes which Daddo took. I scrunched up my eyes, peering at the image. The lorry had none of the dark red markings of those belonging to the estate which arrived late each Friday afternoon to fetch the week's timber. It seemed to me then that it was very important to be quiet. Daddo rapped on the side of the lorry with his hook and it drove off. I waited while he entered the cabin and then I waited another five minutes, but by then it was getting cold.

Inside the cabin, I found Daddo had not gone back to bed, but was crouched rekindling the stove. He heard me enter and looked over his shoulder and seemed about to speak, but I rushed past him into the bedroom. I hadn't yet learned how to deliver a reassuring lie, but I knew enough to sense the wave of suspicion on which I closed the door.

The next time I came to visit, Nana wasn't in the town square to meet me. Later on, it was explained as a misunderstanding over the wires stretching from a telephone box in deep Argyll to our Glasgow flat. But here was a challenge to my independence. I got off the bus quickly and gave one last dutiful look around for

Nana. Then I lifted my suitcase and headed out of town. Soon I
was on the stony track which climbed into the hills on whose lower
slopes the forest began. As I walked I imagined the welcome at the
cabin which would be my reward.

In the past, snug in the green leather passenger seat of the Austin
with Nana driving and talking all the while, the journey had seemed
to take perhaps ten or fifteen minutes. I remembered there was a
turning off the main track to the right which descended into the
forest, the trees immediately closing over our heads, the passageway
feeling almost subterranean, on either side the soft green light
dissolving into the dark.

So when an exit to the right offered itself, I took it. After walking
for another half hour, the track became overgrown and rocky and
it was clear no car had ever driven down it. Although it was late
afternoon, in the depths of the forest it might as well have been
night. Retracing your steps is not a simple matter where there are
trees. Tracks which seem like junctions on the way in, can fork
away from you on the way out. An hour later so little light remained,
I could barely see the trees which surrounded me. I felt my way to
a huge oak and placed my back against it, then slid down to sit on
my suitcase. There was nothing for it but to wait until morning,
listening in the darkness to the sounds from the forest of things
that don't sleep. It was December and it began to snow, the smaller
flakes dodging past branches and settling on the ground. Now I
had stopped walking, I began to feel cold, but it was cold unlike
any I had known before.

The radio that winter had for a week recounted the story of a
party of walkers benighted in a snowstorm on Rannoch Moor and
except for one, all dead by morning. I wondered what it would be
like to die of cold. My father had told me how, as a prisoner during
the war, he had kept up his spirits on a winter march by singing. I
tried to remember the words of a song he used to sing on the rare
mornings he was at home. My mouth opened but instead of the
song, a wordless scream came out which frightened me even more.

For better or for worse, that night I learned the importance in life of a tight seal against such leakage.

I must have drifted into sleep, because I awoke to someone shaking me by the shoulder. At first all I could see in the darkness was a flaring torch held above the stranger's head. It was like something from my picture-book about Robin Hood. The man, dressed in clothes of browns and greens, with a piece of string holding his coat together, and a leather cap on his head, did not speak, but jerked his head upwards. I got to my feet and he lifted my suitcase, taking a few steps before he turned and beckoned me to follow. We left all the visible tracks and plunged deeper into the trees. This was a time before children were taught to distrust all strangers, and it was a time when I, perhaps more than most, still believed in their kindness.

To my surprise it took only a few minutes before we arrived at a clearing in which stood a hooped structure made of branches and covered with tarpaulin. Smoke escaped from a narrow chimney made of iron which stuck out through the roof and this led to a small makeshift stove I spotted as soon as I ducked inside. I stumbled towards it holding out my hands and fell to my knees, letting the warmth seep into every part of me.

'Thank you,' I said to the stranger, who had untied his coat and thrown it in the corner of the room. He did not reply but dipped a small blackened kettle in a bucket of water by the stove and then placed it on top. Soon I was cradling a mug of chocolate. The stranger seemed to not want to speak. Instead he placed a half-finished packet of digestive biscuits within my reach, and draped a blanket around my shoulders. Then he lay down on the only bed and was quickly asleep. I sat beside the stove until my head began to nod and then I curled up on the floor of beaten earth with the blanket over me, as usual with one hand over my mouth and one over my heart.

I awoke in the morning to the smell of oats being cooked. The man gave the pot a last stir and then dumped porridge and milk in a metal bowl and gave it to me. After breakfast he put on his coat, tied it again with string and led the way out of the shelter. Half an hour later we emerged from the trees above the sawmill. Looking back now, it was a mystery that he knew where to take me, because I hadn't told him. I was so relieved to see my grandparents' cabin that I took a couple of steps before turning to thank the man, but already he had disappeared into the trees.

It was early, so all were still sleeping when I knocked on the door of the cabin. Daddo let me in but said nothing, instead calling to Nana and Ross. When we were all assembled in the main room he barked, 'Where the hell have you been?'

I was taken aback, particularly because Nana remained silent, but I told my story. When I came to the end, Daddo snorted. 'A fine tale. What have ye really been up to?'

I didn't know what to say. I looked at Nana who now came forward and put her arm around my shoulders. 'I thought you were coming on the late bus laddie. I'm sorry.' There was something in her voice I hadn't heard before. 'That man. He's the Dummy who used to stay in these woods in the autumn months. Couldna' hear or speak. A tinker. He stayed in a gellie like the one you describe. But lad, he's been dead ten years. He mended our pots once, but died soon after.'

'The boy's a liar, that's what he is,' said Daddo. He turned to Nana. 'I'll bet some of these estate keepers found him and he's been blabbing . . .'

'Och Daddo, don't say that about the lad,' said Nana. Her voice trailed off. 'Maybe the Dummy came back . . .?'

'Oh aye, back from the dead, right enough Lizzie.' He looked me up and down. 'Could be the boy's just like his mother.'

Things were never the same after that morning. Ross and I went to look for the tinker's gellie but I wasn't much help; one clearing looked much like another. When Nana put me on the bus at the end of the week, from her lips came no declamation of vernacular poetry. She paid the bus driver and then handed me a paper bag with the currant buns I loved which she had made that morning.

'Ach laddie,' she said. 'Keep your head in these books and I see you going far.' She tousled my hair, planted a kiss on my cheek, and then she was gone.

Not long after that my father returned from overseas and reviewed our domestic arrangements. A consequence of this for me, was that I was sent to a military boarding school for the sons of servicemen.

I never saw Ross again, but when I eavesdropped on a drunken argument between my father and mother shortly before I departed for the school, something about him was revealed. I had been labelled a liar, but as is often the case, it was the children who were lied to. Ross was not my uncle after all, his mother was not Nana, and his father was an American sailor my mother met on a brief visit to Tarbert. We were half-brothers.

One day at the school, with Christmas approaching, a time when I might well have expected to be placed on the Inveraray bus, I received a letter from my mother. I took it with me to a room high up in one of the faux-gothic towers which stood at each corner of the school. I spread the letter on a desk I favoured because above it was a window which looked west across the barrack square to the snowy ranges of Sheriffmuir. Beyond them I imagined the hills and forests of Argyll.

My mother wrote that my grandparents' sawmill had been broken up, the men paid off and the lorries and cabins sold. They had moved to the city of Perth to work for a timber contractor, where Nana's quick mind was useful in the office, and driving a forklift in the warehouse was easy enough for a man with a hook. There was something else in the envelope. I shook it and a card dropped out from Nana with the verse I have kept with me all my days.

A year ago, I took the bus to Inveraray again, something I had promised myself I would do, but work, marriage and children had got in the way. The children were grown up and away and by then the marriage was over, so there were no more excuses. By early afternoon I walked out of the town on the old track, now covered in tarmac. Taking the correct turning this time, I paused when the track began to descend to the river. It wasn't quite visible, but I knew it was there, because I could hear it, and now and then the sunlight reflected off the dark water curving under the foliage. Fifty years had passed and naturally the forest had seeded many children. These had won back the land on which Ross and I had played and Daddo had milled timber. Nothing could be seen now but trees.

Rob McInroy
FRESH WATTER

The day I heard Jeannie was haein a bairnie I found a beezer of a pearl in the shallows of the Tay. It wid form a rare centre for the necklace I was makin but as I sat lookin at it that nicht, Faither's words birlin in my ears, it fair lost its shine.

'Aye lookin like butter widnae melt in her mooth, the hoor,' Faither said. 'Let that be a lesson tae you. Nivver trust the wenches.'

It was all I could do no tae cry but I'd hae got a hiding for that, so I dug my hen's claw intae my palm tae take my mind aff Jeannie Anderson. She was haein a bairnie. She'd been wi a man. It was a damned, damned shame.

There was a letter sittin on the table and I could see it was frae Geordie Tracey, the coalman. Faither wisnae a big reader and he was waitin for me tae tell him what it said. I stood in front of the windae tae get the light and read it oot. Faither was clatterin aboot wi the range like he wisnae really listenin but I kent fine he was. 'Dear Mr Kelty,' I read, 'I regret to inform you that you owe for three months' coal and as a consequence I will not deliver any more until payment is made.'

'It's nearly summer onyway,' Faither said.

It wasnae that near summer but I didnae argue. 'I'll speak tae the fairmer,' I said, 'and ask him if we can chop some wood.'

'Ye'll do no such thing. And hae Andrew McAlister ken we're hard up? We'll manage.' He opened the range door and threw the letter intae the flames.

'Wee Boab', abody called me at school. Faither was near sixty and didnae let me mix wi other laddies. They werenae couth, he said. So I didnae hae ony friends. I was juist wee auld-fashioned Boab wi his funny words and short breeks and baggy jumper wi patches all ower it.

'It's no my fault,' I wanted tae tell them. 'I'm no that different frae you.' But wee Boab was the butt of abody's jokes. So I kept oot

the way, went doon the Tay wi my glass-bottomed bucket and my
rickety boat and floated on the watter lookin for pearls. Makin
my necklace. A present for a lassie.

A lassie like Jeannie.

It was thinkin aboot Jeannie that got me intae trouble at school.
We were only a wee school, thirty of us, all in one classroom. Jeannie
was fifteen, twa years aulder than me, and she sat at the front, or
at least she did until the bairnie. Noo her seat was empty, for the
Dominie widnae let anyone else sit in it.

'Tarnished,' he said. 'Sullied. She's used goods now. Nobody will
look at her again.' I mind his face when he said that, all stiff like
he was needin a jobbie. I stared at her chair, imaginin her in it, her
thin arms and long, dark hair, the way she curved, those lovely
bosoms. I was in my ain wee world.

'Robert, what did I just say?' shouted the Dominie.

I had nae idea. It was somethin aboot thon Mr Churchill's Gold
Standard that abody was fair vexed aboot. I'm sure it was awfae
important but I couldnae see what it had tae dae wi us in Perthshire.
The Dominie was standin ower my desk and I could smell the
pipe-smoke on his tweed suit. His nose was richt hairy. My heart
started bangin and my haunds were shakin. I'd never got intae
trouble wi the Dominie in my life.

'I'm awfae sorry, sir.'

'Next time I catch you not listening, Robert Kelty, it'll be six of
the strap. Do you hear?'

'Aye sir.'

Abody else heard, too. I was black-affronted as they laughed at
wee Boab gettin intae trouble.

Jeannie had her bairnie in March of 1927. 'That's the only thing
the hussy's got richt,' said Faither. 'All bairnies should be born in
the springtime.'

'I was born in December,' I said and he clouted me that hard
my lug was buzzin for half an hour. He mairched oot tae feed

the cuddies and nae mair was said. Faither had nivver been a man tae laugh much, but since Christmas he'd been richt dowie.

It was a wee laddie Jeannie had, called Jimmy, and a handsome cratur he was, too. She birled him aboot toon maist days in the black pram her mither bocht her in Perth. Abody smiled and cuddled the wee thing, and it seemed tae me that, apart frae the Dominie and Faither, maist folks didnae seem tae mind awfae much aboot Jeannie and her bairnie.

She widnae say wha the faither was, juist smiled and said, 'Jimmy's precious, that's all that matters.' That made the Dominie worse. He forbade any mention of her name. 'Wickedness walks its own path, it needn't concern the righteous,' he said and placed a picter of oor lord Jesus Christ on her auld chair. I asked Faither what for, and he said it was tae purify the air she breathed. She disnae breathe through her arse, I wanted tae say.

But it biled my insides that someone had done it wi Jeannie and I sair needed tae ken wha it was so's I could hate him. I tried hatin abody in toon, but that didnae satisfy. There was nae point in hatin Kenny the butcher – the man was eighty and blund, couldnae hae found his willie let alone use it. So I hated Jeannie instead, her and her bairn and the way she swaggered doon the street like she was a real wifie and no just a fifteen-year-auld lassie lumbered wi a bairn afore her time.

I was countin the days till I could leave school and work on the fairm wi Faither. Tending the heavy horses was a job for life, and I was guid at it already, which was mair than I could say for my schoolin. Whit did I want tae learn yon algebra for, or fancy English? I was fair stupit, I kent that, but I juist behaved mysel and was nae bother, no like the other laddies. Aye, but they all thocht it a grand wheeze tae try tae get me intae trouble. Ae time they left a deid puddock on Miss Massie's desk and blamed it on me. It didnae work, of course, for Miss Massie and the Dominie kent fine I wisnae the sort of laddie tae dae sic a thing.

But ae day they succeeded. Dauvit McTavish was makin a richt clatter at the back of the classroom while the Dominie was writin on the blackboard. The Dominie wisnae a man tae keep his temper lang and I was fell worried.

'Silence!' he shouted. Even though I hadnae done onything I was petrified. 'Any more noise and the whole class will get strapped.'

I knew I was done for. I could see them laughin and pointin at me.

'Wee Boabbie's goin tae get the belt,' Dauvit whispered tae me. I shook my heid, prayin they widnae dae sic a nasty thing.

Aye, but they did.

I think it was Andra McTavish wha farted, a topper that stunk like a rabbit deid in a ditch.

'That's it,' said the Dominie, throwin doon his chalk, ash-faced wi anger. He lined us up, the laddies and the lassies tae, and he strapped us fower times each. I was last and I was near greetin by the time it was my turn. Abody cheered. It hurt like stink.

But that was nothin. What wid Faither say?

I sat on the side of the brae after school and checked my haunds tae see if there was ony bruisin. There wisnae, but Faither would still ken. He'd see it on my face.

'Ye're lookin awfae worried, Bob.'

As if I didnae hae enough tae think aboot, it was Jeannie Anderson. It wisnae that warm, but she was showin mair cleavage than Clara Bow, and I think she had lipsticks on, too. Faither was richt aboot her, the hoor.

She spread her skirt oot and sat doon beside me, plonkin her bairnie on her knee. Funny, once upon a time I'd hae given all my pearls tae hae her sit next tae me, but noo I couldnae be fashed.

'Ach, I was juist wonderin whaur tae get some peewit eggs,' I said.

'As if you wouldn't know where tae get peewit eggs, you livin on a farm.' I felt mysel blush. It was like a warning – I couldnae lee tae save mysel. 'Would it be anythin to do with school that's botherin you?'

'Naw,' I said, ower fast.

'Bob!' She was teasing me, ticklin the bairn tae make it laugh as well. 'Dauvit told me what happened.'

'Well, hae a guid laugh. Abody else has.'

'I'm not laughin. But it's not that serious, is it? It doesn't matter. Abody gets the belt some time. Even wee Jimmy will, one day, won't you, ruffian?'

Silly lassie, bletherin tae her bairn as if bein a mither meant she knew the meanin of aathing. She hadnae seen my faither in a temper. 'If you ever get intae trouble at school,' he'd say, 'I'll thrash ye twice as bad when ye get hame.'

So I put her richt, telt her Faither would beat me black and blue.

'Well, don't tell him.'

'I cannae lee tae my faither.'

'It's not leein, you're just not telling him everything.'

'It's the same thing.'

''Course it's not. You don't tell everybody everything you do.'

'I do my faither, aye.'

'Oh, you've a lot to learn.'

Madam Muck, handin oot the words of wisdom. She wisnae so wise ten months syne, when she was hoikin up her skirt for some cheap bastart that widnae stick by her.

'I'll tell you what,' she said, 'I'll come back with you. Explain to your father. It wasn't your fault.'

'No!' I shouted and I could see she was taken aback.

'Why not?'

I couldnae say that Faither widnae let her within a mile of the fairm. If he knew I'd even been speakin tae her I'd get an even worse beatin. 'It's just my faither,' I said. 'He disnae like me talkin tae girls.'

Jeannie ruffled my hair. 'Bob Kelty, for someone who doesn't lie you tell a right lot of fibs.'

'An for someone who's sic a lot tae tell, you dinnae say awfae much.'

The moment I said it I was terrified. I looked away, like I could pretend I hadnae said it. I'm no one for confrontation. I aye lose. But Jeannie laughed.

'And what do you mean by that?'

I pointed tae the bairn. 'The faither.'

'Like I said, you don't tell everybody everything you do in life.'

I wanted tae argue, but how could I? I hadnae seen ony life.

'Aye well,' she said. 'I'll away home, Jimmy'll be needin his feed.' She cuddled the bairn tae her chest and its heid lolled tae one side. He watched me, his blue eyes all sparkly, juist like his mother's. The pair of them seemed awfae weel suited.

'What does he eat?' I said.

'What d'you think he eats? Why d'you think I've got these?' She shoogled her bosoms and my face burned hotter than a dung heap in August. I could hear her laughin as I ran doon the brae.

Faither was in a mood when I got hame. 'How was school?' he said. He nivver asked me about school. Nivver. School was juist somethin tae be endured and it was of nae interest tae him or me. Why did he hae tae ask today of all days? I didnae answer and he scowled at me. He filled the kettle and stuck it on the range.

'Well?'

I had tae tell him. I kent what Jeannie said made sense but I couldnae dae it. 'I got intae trouble,' I said. 'It wisnae my fault. The hale class got the belt.'

'You got the belt?'

'Aye.'

'How mony?'

'Fower.'

He never said another word, juist walked oot tae the yard tae chop some kindlin. I kent that wisnae the end of it, though, and richt enough when he came back he stripped aff his belt and bent me ower the table and gied me eight strokes across the bahookie.

'I've telt you often enough,' he said, 'if you get intae trouble at school ye'll get it twice as bad frae me.'

He was shakin by the time he'd finished and I felt that guilty I apologised. 'I didnae mean tae disappoint you,' I said.

'We'll say nae mair,' he said but I could tell it was on his mind. He couldnae settle that evenin, up and doon, lookin in cupboards, bangin aboot. He took the shotgun oot of the wardrobe and started cleanin it, which was strange because that was a Sunday nicht job. And when he finished he left it lyin on the kitchen table, which was maist unusual, too, for he was generally richt particular aboot keepin it locked. I watched him quietly. He kept shakin his heid like he was arguin wi himsel. His haunds were shakin. I was sorry for bein sic a trial tae him but all the time I couldnae stop thinkin aboot Jeannie and her bairn. They seemed that happy thigither. The way the wee thing clung tae its mither was a sight tae behold.

Mostly, I nivver minded no haein a mither. It seemed frae whit the other laddies said they spent maist of their time fussin ower you, and at least Faither never did that. I'd nae memories of her, not one, and Faither never spoke aboot her. In fact, there wisnae even a picter of her in the hoose.

Faither had a totty of whisky afore bedtime, which was maist unusual for a Friday, but I didnae mind. He was mair talkative when he'd had a nip and it was nice tae chat tae him man tae man. I dinnae ken what made me ask aboot mither that night – I didnae mean to, it just fell oot my gab.

Faither was silent. He poured himsel anither whisky and sat doon wi last week's *Sunday Post*, pretendin tae read it, but I kent he was goin tae speak. I could tell by the way his left leg was shooglin ower his right.

'Your mither's deid.'

'Aye, but how did she dee? And whit was she like? Was she bonny?' Noo that I'd started, I couldnae stop.

'Whit's past is past. Leave it.'

Maybe I was gettin fu on the fumes of Faither's whisky, or maybe I didnae think I'd get twa beatins in one day, but I kept on at him, long efter I should have stopped.

'Enough!' he shouted. I shrank back in my chair. He could turn awfae fast and when he did you didnae hing aboot. But I was flabbergasted by what happened next.

He started greetin.

My faither. Greetin. I didnae ken whaur tae look. The man was aside himsel, his haunds gripped roond his knees, his heid doon and his body all rigid except for his chest, which was heavin like he'd juist raced Eric Liddell in the hundred yards. I went tae bed no tae embarrass him further.

When I came ben for breakfast the next mornin he was pokin aboot in the cupboards again. I didnae hear him come tae bed and he looked like he hadnae slept. There were bills and papers all ower the table. Finally he let oot a cry and came up wi an auld, tattered envelope.

'Does that say General Accident?' he said.

'Aye.'

He left it on the sideboard and went oot tae chop wood. When I was sure he was gone I had a look. It was a life insurance policy for fifty pounds and I supposed he was goin tae cash it in tae pay the coalman. That was good, onyway. He came back and drapped an armful of logs on the stane floor.

'Ye're goin tae hae tae grow up,' he said.

I was fell upset he was still disappointed in me for gettin the belt. 'Aye,' I said. 'Sorry.'

When I finished my chores I went doon the river tae look for pearls. I'd been there maybe an hour when I saw Jeannie by the watterside.

'Hello,' she said. 'I didn't see you there, with yer head in that bucket.'

'Best way tae find pearls.'

'Aye? And who would you be collecting pearls for?'

I turned the boat tae shore and I dinnae think she noticed me blushin. We sat by the riverbank and I explained all aboot the

pearl fishin. It's no complicated but she seemed fair impressed.
Aye, but she was easy company. I'm no awfae sure wi people, bein
a bit of a dunderheid, but Jeannie was a couthy lass and she made
me feel braw.

'Why do you keep looking over my shoulder?' she said, laughin.
'Are you worried somebody might see us together?'

I tried tae deny it but she laughed even more.

'My faither,' I heard mysel sayin. The truth juist falls oot my
mooth sometimes.

'Your faither? Does he not approve of me?'

'Naw.' There was nae point denying it.

'Well let me tell you, Bob Kelty, wee Jimmy's the best thing
that's ever happened to me. I look into his eyes and what do I see?
I hold him and what do I feel? I dream about him. I wake up in
the morning and rush to his cot to look at him. Just look at him. I
feel him all cosy against me, his wee hand curled against mine.
Eyes staring into mine. And I see what he's thinking. It's plain on
his face. He's thinking I'm his mother and he loves me.

'Isn't that the most special thing you could ever imagine?'

Jeannie's eyes were shiny wi tears. Jings, first Faither, noo her.

'Dinnae you start,' I said.

'Start what?'

'Greetin.'

'Why? Who else has been greetin?' Suddenly, she became the
bossy besom again and I was juist wee Boab and she widnae let up.
'Who else has been greetin on you? Tell me. Tell me.'

In the end, I gave in. 'Faither,' I said.

'Your faither!'

'Wheesht.'

'Your faither was greetin? Why?'

I found mysel explainin aathing, aboot my mither, how he
wouldnae talk aboot her. How much I wanted tae ken aboot her.
It was a fell relief, for I'd been thinkin aboot it all morning.

'The poor man,' she said.

I was amazed. I was expectin sympathy for me, no him. 'Come aff it,' I said.

'What?'

'Jings, the man's juist like you. There's you, winnae say onythin aboot the faither of that bairn. And there's Faither, winnae speak a word aboot my mither. Whit's the difference? Ye cannae say 'poor man' aboot him when ye're daein the same thing yersel.'

She smiled. 'Aye, maybe. But there's a right time and a wrong time for telling, and a right reason and a wrong one. I'll probably never speak about it, and I have my reasons. But I'm not your father, I can't speak for him.'

'I tell ye, it's ower complicated, this growin up. Sometimes ye should, sometimes ye shouldnae. Wha's tae ken?'

Jeannie smiled. Jimmy started tae greet and she draped him ower her chest and patted his back.

'He'll be needin a feed,' I said.

'Aye, I'd best be off home.'

She looked smashin. She seemed tae glow wi the mitherhood. 'You could do it here,' I said. 'There's naebody aboot.'

'Except you.'

'Och, I widnae mind.'

'Would ye not?'

I didnae ken what I was feelin, juist then. It was like I was goin tae be sick. There were too many thochts in my heid for my stupit brain tae manage. I wanted tae ken aboot my mither but I'd nae way of findin oot. I thocht aboot Faither, greetin intae his whisky. I thocht about the Dominie, plonkin a picter of Jesus Christ on Jeannie's chair. Callin her 'used goods'. Well, it seemed tae me Jeannie and her bairnie were juist grand. I could see their love. Feel it.

I wanted it.

'No, Jeannie,' I said. 'It's no right tae hide things.'

She smiled. She nodded and began to unbutton her blouse. It was the maist beautiful thing I ever saw.

As I walked hame afterwards wi my bucket empty and my heid fu, I thocht aboot Faither tellin me I'd hae tae grow up. Well, I thocht, I wisnae a wee laddie any more now.

Aye, so's I thocht.

The door was locked when I got hame. It was never locked. I didnae hae a key. I walked roond the back and keeked in the kitchen windae.

'Faither?' I shouted.

But I kent already Faither wasnae goin tae answer.

Carol McKay
HER BODY WAS AN AVIARY

> . . . *she already knew how to fly: by now at night she dreamt of nothing else* . . .
> —Primo Levi, 'The Great Mutation', *The Mirror Maker* (Minerva, 1991). Translated from the Italian by Raymond Rosenthal.

Emma hadn't been right since the man came.

Now, she and Mo were sitting on the sofa: Nihal on the radio, the sun well up in the sky. She tugged Mo's arm, because he wasn't even listening. 'I've got a temperature.'

His eyes remained fixed on his phone.

'Feel it.'

He freed his arm from her grip and took a long look at her, his dark eyebrows meeting in the middle. 'You've a runny nose and a sore throat. It's hardly bird flu.'

She thumped her body into the sofa. 'But feel!'

At last he skimmed the backs of his fingers off her forehead. 'Take a couple of pills for it.'

'Could you get me some? At the shops?' She squeezed out two feeble coughs and pulled her feet up. They were pink and bare with the nails painted orange to match the stripe in her hair. *My bird of paradise*: that's what he called her. She was wearing her black and orange onesie and a scarlet towelling bath robe. He said he'd bought that specially for her, though she found a paper hankie in a pocket. 'Please?'

He jabbed a finger into her upper arm. 'The things I do for you!'

'Ouch!'

He lifted her foot and kissed it. 'Why are there no pills in the jungle?'

'Yeah, yeah.' It was an old one. 'The *parrots eat 'em all.*'

'That joke doesn't work in Canada, did you know? They call it Tylenol there.'

'Just as well they don't have bird flu, then,' Emma said, and closed her eyes.

Mo had travelled. That was one of the things she liked about him. He had done so many interesting things. Not like her. She'd stayed all her life in this one little town. She was going to travel – as soon as she hit sixteen. Or sooner, with Mo, if he'd take her.

She cleared her throat again. 'Will you go and get me some? Otherwise I think I'm going to die from this.' She rubbed her hands over her lower abdomen, the memory of what the man did not forgotten.

'Drama queen!' he said, and stood up. 'Can you lend me a fiver?'

'I've only got the tenner you gave me.'

He pushed his hands into his pockets and turned over the change. 'In that case, can I take a tenner?'

She went to bed and dreamed she was flying. The sky was light blue above her, deeper behind her, and, at the horizon she was flying towards, wispy clouds glowed blue-black, with a halo of golden rays. High in the sky, she felt liberated from the heavy dragging feeling. She felt buoyed on rising air. She held her arms out to let the warm wind flow over her breast-bone, under her arms and all along her body and legs. It was the lightest she'd felt since . . .

'Good morning,' Mo said.

She opened her eyes to see him leaning over her. For a moment she thought he was a brown feathered buzzard, but he was an ordinary man with a glass of water in his hand.

'You were sound,' he said. 'You okay? I brought you up another couple of Paracetamol.'

She leaned on one elbow, took the pills and swallowed them. He'd let the water run till it was cold and she relished the cool flow of it inside her gullet.

He sat on the edge of the bed, dressed in his brown pullover with the cream Fair Isle pattern below the V-neck, and skinny jeans, watching her. 'I think you'll need to give yourself a day or two to

get over this,' he said. He ran his hand through her hair then stopped
at something.

'What is it?'

'Just a crumb or something.'

Her hair was thick and long and must be tangled. She couldn't
remember when she'd last brushed it. Mo pulled up a lock and let
hairs drift on to her cheek while he tried to isolate what he'd spotted
in the strands. He breathed a soft laugh. 'Maybe you *have* got bird
flu. Look.' He held up a small white feather. 'Then again, it's probably
just feather-pillow-itis.' He let it fall into the bin beside the bed
then laid his hand on her shoulder, his thumb caressing her cheek.
'Stay in bed for a while, okay? Shout me when you're peckish.'

'I don't want anything,' she said, her voice breaking. 'I'm not
hungry.'

'But you have to eat, Em. You know you have to eat. Starving
yourself won't get you back in shape.' He stroked her cheek some
more. 'The pills'll help. And don't forget your water.'

He kissed her hair, the sound smacking in her ear, then went
downstairs again. Later, she heard the hoover. He must be worried
if he was doing the hoovering. Or maybe his mates were coming.
Though surely not with her poorly.

She spent the morning between sleep and wakefulness, flitting
from one to the other till she didn't know which was real. She
dreamt, again, that she was flying, but this time in rhythmic
formation with others, forming the two arms of a long V-shape.
She woke to the drum of seagulls on the roof.

Her throat felt dry. She dreamt she was a goose being force fed
through a funnel. She woke retching, and reached a shaky hand
towards her glass. She lost all track of time. Then she dreamt she
was darting through water, sleek and slender, breaking the surface
with a fish in her mouth and scattering water droplets from her
plumage to dot the surface with spots and ripples.

Maybe she called out. Mo's heavy tread sounded on the stairs.
'Hiya,' he said, massaging her shoulder. 'Want something to eat?'

'No.'

He brought her a sandwich, cut into triangles with the crusts removed the way she liked it, and stayed with her while she ate a few bites then lay down again. He turned her hand over between his and nuzzled her fingertips, his black beard and his mouth soft on her skin. 'How are you now?'

'I dreamt I was flying. It was really nice.' She thought for a minute. 'Remember I told you Mrs Johnstone read us a story?'

He traced the outline of her lips with his finger. 'You stayed at school long enough to hear a story?'

'It was about a girl my age who turned into a bird.' She caught his hand and held it to her cheek. 'She got an itchy back and a fever, and when her mum felt her shoulder blades, they were covered in feathers. Maybe I'm turning into a bird. Maybe that's why I'm dreaming of flying.'

'You're hilarious,' Mo said. 'Give us a feel.' Nimble, he climbed on the bed, one knee on each side of her, and raised her upper body. She didn't protest so he moved a hand down the back of her onesie and slid it around over her shoulder blades. 'No feathers there,' he said, voice low. Emma twisted, giggled weakly then lay back while he held her. He kissed her mouth, and cheeks, and eyelids.

'I'm not well, Mo,' she whispered. 'You've made my heart go all fluttery.'

'I know,' he whispered back. 'I have that effect on birds.' He kissed her. 'Don't worry, I'm not pushing you. Just giving a little TLC.'

'Give us a cuddle,' she said. When he lay down, she nestled into his chest and closed her eyes.

'Do you love me?' she asked.

'Of course I do.'

'And I'm your bird of paradise?'

'The one and only.'

He squeezed her. 'You seem brighter,' he said. 'I might get my mates round for a flying visit later.'

*

An almighty quivering in her ribcage woke her. Her body felt like an aviary filled with doves. There were wisps of something tickling her windpipe, sucking up all the moisture and thickening on the insides of her lips. She opened her mouth to call but no noise escaped. 'Mo!' she tried again, still with no sound issuing. She reached for the water glass but knocked it over. He must have heard it hit the laminate floor, because he ran upstairs.

'Calm!' he said, head round the door.

She struggled to wet her throat, panicky. 'You need to get me a doctor.'

'You're fine!' he said. 'Calm down!' He filled the glass from the en-suite tap, held it so she could sip from it then moved it away again. 'There's white stuff on your mouth.' He dabbed it with a tissue from the bedside box. Brows lowered, he passed the glass back. 'Drink it all,' he said.

'I need antibiotics.'

'Don't make such a fuss.' He got a text and took his phone out of his pocket to read it.

'I don't want your mates round.' Her hand shook as she passed him the empty glass. 'I'm not ready.' She pulled a strand of hair from her lips. 'I think something went wrong, Mo. When the man came. You need to get me a doctor.'

He scowled and put his phone back in his pocket. 'Nothing went wrong!' he said, and glared at her. 'Nothing. Do you hear me?'

She whined. 'You made my heart go all fluttery again.'

'Take two pills and sleep it off.' He pulled the bedroom door shut behind him, all the way till it clicked.

*

She must have fallen asleep again. She thought she heard the front door close and the car pull away but that might have been yesterday. A phone rang, and there was a car alarm. A magpie made a rattling noise, haranguing a cat. There was a long spell of silence.

She drifted between sleep and wakefulness. The covers were over her face and she struggled to free herself, forced down by something heavy. There was a violent beating and something metal-sharp gripped at her, producing a raw, tearing sensation. A massive darkness towered in the space between bed and ceiling, wings beating, sweeping dust and fine down on either side into a vortex. No, that was a memory. It lasted only a moment and was followed by a long term of sun-dappled light.

Sometimes Mo was there, her huge brown bird with the cream-coloured V down his chest and his wide wings outstretched. Sometimes she was alone with her eyes on the sky, which was as blue as it had been in her dream; in one of her dreams. She was burning. She threw back the cover and undid the zip of her onesie. Her belly felt huge. It must be swollen with all the water she'd been drinking. It was swollen and gurgling. Waves rolled over its surface. Then came an urge to bear down. She pushed down the fleecy onesie and freed her limbs, revelling in the air so cool on her skin. The urge to push came again, overpowering. She drew her knees up and gave in to it. She pushed until the instinct abated.

She slid her fingers between her legs and felt something smooth and hard, stretching her vulva beyond anything she'd imagined possible, as if she had a football in her vagina. Hot and moist, it bulged, hard and damp, swelling to fill more space down there than she knew existed. Her hand came away red. Was she delirious? Had she been ill so long she'd spent nine months sleeping? Again came the urge: irresistible. She pressed her chin to her chest, gripped the backs of her thighs, and squeezed. It must be the baby. Hers, and Mo's baby. They hadn't got rid of it. She hoped it was Mo's baby. She felt it move down inside her – the strangest sensation – then with another great surge it burst free and the relief was instantaneous. The widest part of it was free and the rest slithered out, hot on the insides of her thighs. She must've had a baby. Yet when she looked, it wasn't a baby but an egg: a huge, wet, reddish-brown egg. *My bird of paradise,* he'd called her. She lifted it, curious, astonished at the off-centre balance of it; lifted it to her mouth feeling overwhelming love for it; transferred its heat to the skin around her lips, before, shuddering, she reached with one hand to draw up the quilt again, to keep both her and her baby warm and safe: to incubate it.

*

When she woke the room was in darkness, with little stripes of light lining the edges of the curtains. Lying on her right side, she became aware of Mo's warmth behind her, his arm over her waist and the egg she was holding close to her stomach. But the egg had cooled. The quilt was over her, and over it, but the egg was almost cold.

'It's dead!' she cried, clutching it to her chest.

Mo flicked the lamp switch. Bleary, he asked what she was talking about.

'It's dead!'

'It's a fucking hot water bottle, Em! Look at it!'

And there it was, plump red rubber.

And in a moment of clarity she remembered how angry Mo had been, and the man who had peeled back her covers and put the plastic sheet under her buttocks; who shone the lamp between her legs and poked his fingers then sharp things into her while Mo stood watching in the half-light, arms crossed on his chest and his mouth twisted. Such an ache in her belly! Worse than any cramp. She heard their subdued conversation while she shook and shuddered. Saw Mo pass him an envelope then usher him out, leaving her crying. When Mo came back in, he was nice to her. He was kind to her: *my bird of paradise*. The only one who was ever nice to her. And all she wanted now was to get rid of it, get rid of this stupid hot water bottle, and the anguish, to hug into Mo's chest and fall asleep.

'I'm sorry, Mo,' she whimpered.

'What are you like? Stupid bitch. Come here.'

He put out the lamp – the same one the man had shone on her – and lay on his back, his arm round her, pulling her against him, and she, mouth against his black chest hair, fell asleep and dreamt she was a fledgling, pecking and scratching its way out of a hard white shell then flying through the window between the emerald green curtains, up into the sky.

Mark McLaughlin
SINCE I SAW THE SEA

I watched through the windscreen. A rainy Hogmanay, the slap
and sluice of the windscreen wipers. The Clyde Tunnel approached.
My brother and I readied ourselves to hold our breath as we always
did, as every Glasgow kid did going under the tunnel. It usually
took a minute or so to get to the other side. I breathed in deep and
felt the tightness start to build against my lungs. A closeness, a
pressure, moving with each second from chest to neck to head. We
were almost through when the traffic slowed. Daylight just beyond
us, but I could hold no more and breathed out with a sigh. My
brother held still, cheating I'm sure.

The traffic eventually moved, and we headed towards to the A77.
On towards Girvan, on to Aunt Anne and Uncle Emir's. Anne was
my mother's sister and we always spent New Year there. Christmas
at ours, New Year at Anne's. I loved it there, even the journey.
Looking beyond my dad at the wheel, straining for that first sight,
first sound, first smell of the sea.

Preparations were already in full flow when we got there. Anne
met us at the gate, drying her hands on her apron. We hurried
upstairs to leave our bags. I stopped briefly at the bedroom window,
knowing that if I looked between two of the houses opposite, I
could just make out the grey rock of Ailsa Craig in the Firth of
Clyde. I knew that just a few minutes beyond the house lay the
beach. A crescent of grey sand made into a small bay by a low
promontory of rocks. Andy's Bay, Emir called it. *Same name as
you.* He was Turkish Cypriot and had told me the bay he swam in
as a child was called St Andrew's. Even in the coldness of December
it felt so exciting to be so near the sea.

We ran downstairs to the living room. Emir was busy rearranging
furniture so everyone could dance later. He met us open-armed
as always, pulled us close. We helped him and my cousin Marie
pull the chairs against the wall, move the dining table. Some banners

were put up beside the Christmas decorations. *Happy New Year!* and *1985* in big tinsel letters. Soon the room was ready.

Marie and I then played some Monopoly upstairs in her bedroom for a while before we got bored. I started to head back downstairs but passed the bathroom where the door was open. Emir stood there in his vest, getting ready for the party. I watched him wipe the steam from the bathroom mirror. His arms taught and brown as harbour rope. He saw me, caught me eyeing his watch on the edge of the sink and passed it over to me. I hurried to fix the strap, to feel it weighing heavy and hanging loose around my wrist. My dad never let me touch his watch. *Sure, you'll break it.* As he shaved, Emir gurned towards me in the mirror, me laughing away. He towelled his face, winced slightly as he splashed on *Tabac*. He turned then to the hair; his black comb and *Murray's* pomade. He was a huge Elvis fan and his elbows would angle high above his head as he worked the pomade through his hair until it resembled a high D.A. His lips curled in an *uh-huh*. Aunt Anne shouted for him.

'Emir are you still in that bathroom?' she called. 'I need your help down here.'

'Coming now, Precious!' he said. I started to giggle as he rolled his eyes and then hammed it up as *The King*, his comb as a microphone.

'Ladies and gentlemen, Elvis has left the bathroom.'

I followed him downstairs, the tangle of curls from the back of his head already moving free from the pomade.

*

By early evening the door seemed to be going constantly as friends, family and neighbours arrived, the smell of winter on their coats. Marie and I took our place beneath the buffet table, sitting with plates of sausage rolls and crisps, polystyrene cups fizzing with Irn Bru. The conversation grew louder through the night. My brother stood talking to one of the neighbour's daughters. We watched him blush as Marie and I blew kisses towards him. Soon the music grew louder than the chatter; Abba, Neil Diamond, Wham. Elvis whenever they let Emir near the stereo. Marie and I watched the shuffling of feet for a few minutes as everyone started to dance, but soon we took our place on the hallway stairs. She picked up her parents' wedding photograph from the hallway table and stared at it. I watched the statue of St Bernadette which always stood beside it. Her small hands clasped in prayer. The year before I'd told Marie that sometimes, in the winter half-light of the hallway, I felt I saw the statue's head turn towards me. *It's a calling, Andy, it's a calling from God* she'd said. Christ, if I hadn't been scared before I was then. I turned back to Marie, still staring and smiling at the picture.

'See this photo,' she said. 'I pure love it, so I do.'

She was always so full of the romance of her parents' wedding. She'd tell me again and again the stories of how they'd met in London when Aunt Anne was doing nursing training. The parties they threw, the songs he sung her. How they were so broke that they had their wedding reception in their tiny Whitechapel apartment. They placed their hi-fi speakers on the windowsill, and everyone climbed through to dance on the flat roof of the grocery store below them. Dancing while an East End sunset gave way to the flicker of tealight candles and starlight. Dancing like that was all there was. Marie always gushed over the photographs, the colours faded into the dullness of oranges, browns and yellows. But I'd noticed how Grandad and Grandma weren't in any of the photographs and I'd done the maths. I knew that Anne already had Marie in her belly.

We went back into the living room just as the countdown to midnight took place. *5-4-3-2-1!* Then there were party poppers and kisses, hugs and handshakes. Women I didn't know kissed my cheeks, the smell of perfume and cigarettes. Men ruffled my hair. I found my brother to say Happy New Year, but he was kissing the neighbour's daughter in the kitchen, their heads twisting in small, awkward circles. Marie and I just giggled and ran off.

Soon we were sent to say our goodnights. As I waited to speak, I watched Emir, my dad and some other men talking.

'So, what . . . you even swim there in winter?' asked Dad.

'A quick dip every day,' said Emir. 'I've done it my whole life, from growing up in Northern Cyprus, to lidos in London and now here.'

'But you swim here in the sea?' asked another man.

Emir nodded.

'Even on New Year's morning?' asked Dad.

'Every day.'

I approached my dad then. *Night, son* before he turned back to his whisky and the other men. Emir squeezed my shoulders softly.

'Uncle Emir,' I said. 'Could I come with you to the beach? Just to watch.'

'Of course, you can,' he said. 'But it will be early in the morning.'

I lay down on the blow-up mattress on Marie's bedroom floor. I could still hear the throb of music and laughter, dancing footsteps. I thought of the hours until I'd see the sea but soon, I fell asleep.

*

I woke the next morning to light from the hallway creeping beneath the bedroom door. I could hear someone moving in the kitchen, so dressed and hurried downstairs. Emir was rolling up his trunks in a dark blue towel and gathering his bag.

'Morning, Andy,' he said. 'You want some tea?'

I nodded. He still took his tea Turkish style. I watched him pour from the double kettle pot into small glasses. The tea iron-red, floral steam rising. It was bittersweet, so hot it burned my lips. He sat there quietly, smoking the day's first cigarette. I watched him drain the last of his cup. Then I waited for him to turn away and emptied my tea down the sink.

With our coats pulled tight, we quietly made our way down to the beach. The sky sat somewhere between night and morning. Pale orange and faded blue with the sun risen, yet a smattering of

stars just visible, stillborn and glistening above. Emir laid his
duffle coat down on the beach, gestured for me to sit down. My
hands rested against the cool, compact sand. Emir started to
undress, pulling his jumper, shirt and vest off as one. Dark rosary
beads hung around his neck. I remember thinking how he never
joined us at Mass. He pulled the beads over his head and placed
them and his watch in my hand. Then turned away from me as he
pulled his trousers over his blue bony arse and quickly pulled up
his trunks. Just a brief *God, but it's cold* before he hurried across
the sand. I watched him move towards the waves, rubbing his
palms together. Just the slightest hesitation at the water; as cold
sea reached knee, balls and waist, before his shoulders rose and
he dived into the cresting surf. He swam onwards, his long arms
clawing and ploughing at the slate-coloured water. He looked so
small against the great bowl of morning sky and the granite of
Ailsa Craig in the distance before him. I watched those arms and
feet breaking the surface of the sea, his head twisting to the left to
gulp in cold air.

He seemed to be in the water longer than I'd expected, more
than a *quick dip*. I held the rosary beads tighter. The Church had
its hold on me then and I started to mumble a Hail Mary against
the coldness of morning. By now Emir was so far out that he
barely seemed to be moving. I dropped the rosary beads and
watch into the pocket of his jacket, stood up and walked nervously
towards the water's edge. The thinning of the sea foamed against
my trainers as it reached across the sand, so I stood further back.
Emir still hadn't turned around. I looked about the beach anxiously,
hoping to find someone, anyone, maybe an adult walking their
dog. Someone who could tell me what to do. I called out towards
him, my voice lost against the sound of the surf and the cawing
cries of some seagulls. I thought to walk towards town, find a
phone box and call the police. But what if he did come back and
we lost each other? I waited a moment longer and then started to

edge along the thin line of rocks which reached out towards the sea. In my mind I could walk to the point where maybe I was level with him, or at least he could hear me. The rocks were as jagged as I remembered from summer, but darker and slicker with rain, sea and moss. I tried to balance myself as I walked along, the waves pushing a little further across the rocks towards me with each step. This had seemed like a game when we walked here last summer, flicking stones against the surf and pretending to push each other in. It felt different now. I stopped a moment to see if I could find Emir. I called again but it was hard to shout and stay steady on my feet. To my side the waves seemed stronger now, the water darker, deeper. I thought to turn back but as I did a wave passed straight across my feet and ankles, filling my trainers with sea water.

I tried to turn around but lost my footing and fell backwards into the water. A muffled roar in my ears, the water fizzed, ice-cold around my face. I pushed my head up, my arms and legs frantically splashed to try to keep myself afloat. My head would slip below the surface whenever a wave crossed, but even when I was above the water I struggled to breathe. Feeling again that tightness, that pressure but this time I could do nothing. I looked around, unsure of whether I was facing sea or rock or land. I tried to call for Emir, but the words wouldn't form in my mouth. I felt again a wave crossing cold across my face, pushing me round like I was the smallest piece of driftwood, but then I felt something else. An arm around my chest pulling me onto my back. Emir.

'It's okay,' he said. 'It's okay.'

I couldn't see him, could just feel his arm around me which I held tightly, the sound of his breathing over the slapping of the surf. After a moment I could breathe easier. He kept moving back towards the shore and I just looked up towards the sky. When we made the beach, it felt even colder when I moved free of the water. We hurried to his towel, quickly dried ourselves. He put my wet clothes in his bag, gave me his jumper and wrapped his duffle coat around me. I moved across the sand, legs bare, the coat almost trailing on the ground, the sleeves hanging low beyond my hands. We climbed onto the sea wall and he stopped me, pulled me onto his back. My arms held tight around his neck as we walked. I stared at the back of his head. His hair, more dishevelled than ever, a silver sprinkling of stubble just visible across his cheeks. He walked on, both of us silent, but then the silence was always okay around Emir.

Robbie MacLeòid
GUN BHREITH

a nighean, mo nighean,
bha thu gu bhith nighean
d' athar. sheallainn ort
a' turraman mun cuairt
ruadhag am measg guirmead
an fheòir, làmhan beaga
a' greimeachadh air stocan nam flùr,
fo sgàil na craoibhe malpais.
annas sgàrlaid thu.

faileas do chasan air mo dhà ghualainn
a' teannachadh, is tu a' sealltainn
bho àirde fuamhaire

a' gàireachdainn
sunnd saor, solas buidhe
na grèine, gruag
ruadh, air neo,
's dòcha nach biodh,

is gàire, gàire
do mhàthar,
carach, glacadh
mo chridhe. cha bhithinn
air dhìochuimhneachadh.

bha mi 'g obair air d' òran-tàlaidh
ach uaireannan falbhaidh nithean leis an t-sruth.

UNBORN

you were (to be) a daddy's girl.
I'd watch you teeter along –
little taller than the grass
– wee hands on the dandelions
and the maple tree.
a bright red anomaly.

ghost of your legs on my shoulders,
clung on tight, looking out
from a giant's height.

giggling mirth
yellow sunshine
little redhead
(or not).

just a smile,
your mam's half-smirk.
it was (to be)
never forgotten,
unlost.

I've been working on your lullaby
but sometimes these things slip away.

Thomas Malloch
THE ANATOMY LESSON

When I was young, I was always asking about it.

'What happened to your hand?'

And in his thick Austrian accent, he would say, 'I lose it in the war.'

'But how?'

And he'd shrug his shoulders. 'Such things happened then.'

Always the same patient response. Not like Mum.

'I already told you, *I-don't-know.* Ask again and I'll send you to your room.'

Dad was more like Grand-dad. 'A lot of bad things happened in the war. If he doesn't want to talk about it, we should respect that, don't you think?'

And I would nod and be quiet. Until the next time I passed his open door and he had his stump cover off.

*

He nearly always left his door open, even at night. He said he didn't like the feeling of being closed in which I kind of understood since I always slept with my door open and the hall light on.

Most of the time his stump and cover were hidden in the sleeve of his cardigan. But there were days when his hand hurt, he said, and he had to rub some cream into the skin at the end of his arm. I didn't understand how a hand that wasn't there could hurt but he said that sometimes the nerves jangled and that fooled the brain into thinking that the hand was still there. He didn't know if the rubbing with cream helped but it gave him something to do.

If he didn't notice I was there, I could stare. His forearm was child-thin and hairless and shiny and white, like Mum's best porcelain. Or polished bone. And then the shock of the scar. A puckered zig-zag, like something on a butcher's block.

He spent most of his time in his room.

When he wasn't sleeping or rubbing cream into his stump, he was painting. Flowers mostly. But one afternoon he had a Brussels sprout plant, pulled from the garden, on his work table. All green leaves and dark rootlets. I watched him, bent over, his artist's hand resting on his cardiganed stump as he painted. Slow. Deliberate. Frequent pauses.

His brush had a slender handle and a narrow point of bristles, good for fine detail. The palette was an assortment of greens. Forest, olive, jade, sage and some shades yet to be named.

The painted plant looked so real it might easily have been taken for a photograph.

'Why are you painting vegetables?'

He paused, put the brush down and turned. He had flecks of green paint on his spectacle lenses. Maybe that was what drew my eye. His eyelid droop was heavy and above the rims of his glasses, dark eyebrows were showing wisps of grey. It was a moment of lucidity. Grand-dad was old.

'It is work. I am what is called an illustrator. I do drawings and paintings for book publishers. Mostly flowers, but this,' and he pointed to the painting, 'is for a book on garden vegetables.'

'Why don't they just take photographs?'

He took off his glasses and put them on his lap and rubbed his eyes. 'I don't know. I don't ask.' He picked up the glasses, raised them to his mouth and breathed on them, then back to his lap. He wiped the lenses with a corner of his cardigan. 'They pay. I paint.'

'Do you get a lot of money?'

He looked around the room and smiled. 'No. But it's enough.'

'Maybe you should do something else, then.'

'I'm too old to learn new things. Besides, I like what I do.' He stood up and stretched. 'Though sometimes I think it would be nice to paint other things.'

'Like what?'

'People. I'm good at people.'

'So why don't you?'

'Paint people? No. Nobody wants that anymore.' He sat back down again. 'Now if you will excuse me, I need to finish my painting.'

*

Even a child's curiosity will die without the stimulus of answers. By the time I went to medical school, I was out of the habit of stopping at his door, staring at his withered forearm, asking questions. And he had nothing to ask of me. Until I came home for a visit one weekend near the end of my final year.

'Do you have career plan?'

'I was thinking, surgery. Yes,' I nodded. 'I think I'd like to be a surgeon.'

'You should learn from the best. Find a good anatomy department. Work always with the professor if you can. A good surgeon must know anatomy. Before all else. When time comes, let me know. I will find you the best book.'

And he did. Pernkopf's *Atlas of Human Anatomy* in two volumes. Second-hand. I don't know where he got it.

He opened one of the volumes at an illustration of the back of a human hand. The skin was reflected to show the underlying anatomy, the veins in vivid blues, the arteries scarlet of course, and the nerves in yellow. It looked more like electrical wiring than human tissue.

'Notice the colours. Very bright. Of course these structures are not really so, but this clarity is good for learning. The anatomical accuracy is exceptional. It has never been bettered. Pernkopf was an excellent professor. And he used only the finest artists.'

He'd never been so articulate.

He gazed on the hand.

'Beautiful, no?' He seemed more affected than I could ever remember.

'Yes.' It was all I could think to say.

'Mine, you know.'

*

Pernkopf became my companion, first at the dissecting table, then in my surgical training and finally in my theatre suite when I made consultant. My regard for the precision and beauty of the plates grew with my experience. Whenever I came across an unusual anatomical variant, the atlas showed me how to approach the surgery with exactitude and safety. Naturally, I became curious about a possible relationship between Pernkopf and my grandfather but my visits home were brief affairs and any preliminary comments were met with familiar avoidance tactics.

Then, in the summer of 1995 came two significant events which forever coloured my relationship with the atlas.

A colleague alerted me to a paper by Edzard Ernst. It detailed the Nazi takeover of the University of Vienna, in which Pernkopf was a key figure. It also speculated that university staff had been involved in human experimentation and in the acquisition of the bodies of executed political prisoners.

I made arrangements to visit my parents with the intention of confronting my grandfather with this new information but on the evening before my departure, my father phoned. Grand-dad had been admitted to hospital. A stroke.

*

Dad was at the bedside. He was holding Grand-dad's hand between his two. He placed the hand carefully on the bed and leaned forward.

'Look Dad. It's Max. Come to visit you.'

Grand-dad turned towards me. Right facial droop. A second or two to focus. Then up with his left arm, his stump arm, in salute. No words. I looked at his hand. Motionless.

Dad gave me a hug, then brought a chair in from the corridor. We sat and made conversation. Mum was at home. Busy with a chicken broth. To be made thick for easier swallowing. My journey? Good. No, no delays. Grand-dad was looking better after a good night's sleep, Dad thought. A twitch from the left side of the patient's mouth.

And then some necessary nursing duties. So, Dad and I went for a coffee at the canteen.

'This isn't the first time,' he said. 'Your grand-dad had something similar two months ago.'

'And you didn't tell me?'

'He asked us not to.'

'So he didn't lose his speech *then*?'

'Well, no . . . I mean it went. But he recovered. Less than twenty-four hours, in fact. It was afterwards that he asked us not to contact you.'

'Why?'

'Because he had things he wanted to say to me first.'

'Oh . . . What things?'

And Dad began with stuff that I knew. That his mother had died giving birth to him. That he was an only child. That his father, my grandfather, had doted on him. That Grand-dad had secured a position as an illustrator, the working hours of which were suitable for a single parent.

And then the things I didn't know, the things Dad only found out a matter of months before me. That Grand-dad's position was in the University of Vienna. The Botanical Studies department. That his artistry attracted the attention of other illustrators in other departments. That some of these other illustrators worked for Professor Pernkopf. That my grandfather contributed some illustrations to Pernkopf's collection.

Mine you know.

For a short time we were in our own thoughts. Then I looked at him, eyes down, mug between two hands, coffee untouched.

'Is there more?'

A rueful smile. 'Oh, yes.'

Pernkopf had been a Nazi Party member since 1933. By the Anschluss, he was also dean of the medical school. He used his

position to insist that all medical staff swear an oath of loyalty
to Hitler. Those who refused, were dismissed.

'What about Grand-dad?'

'Well, he wasn't sacked.'

'But he wasn't actually on the medical staff, either.'

'No.'

'So, he might not have been asked to swear.'

'Possibly not. But I really didn't feel like asking.'

Would I have asked?

'Go on,' I said.

'Your grandfather was eligible for military service.'

'Which was when he lost his hand?'

'Kind of.' Dad grimaced. 'But he never served.'

'Then how—'

'It was self-inflicted.'

'What?'

It wasn't a Faustian pact exactly, but a grim one all the same.
The anatomists needed body parts for their research; to keep his
son safe, Grand-dad needed to avoid conscription.

Mine you know.

We made our way back along the corridor.

'Why now?' I said.

Dad stopped, looked at me.

'Such sings vill out.' A fair impression. We both smiled. 'Also,
I think the mini-stroke was a warning. If he didn't speak now,
he might lose the opportunity altogether and risk us finding out
about *such things* from other sources. He preferred that we hear
from him first.'

'We?'

'He was going to tell you this weekend.'

*

Coincidence that he should decide to speak out just as the University
of Vienna's murky past was coming under examination? Probably.

Papers in medical journals rarely broke into the public domain back then. Certainly Ernst's didn't, though it rumbled about in the medical press for a while.

I banished Pernkopf to the back of my locker, unwanted and unneeded for the next year or more. Yet I couldn't bring myself to throw the atlas out. Such exactitude. Such artistry. But the history. The manner in which the bodies were acquired.

Grand-dad never recovered from his stroke. His last months were spent in a nursing home, punctuated by recurrent chest infections, one of which proved terminal. I visited him just before his death. He had a priest in attendance. *The Anointing of the Sick,* I was told. Another insight to Grand-dad's past. We were never church attenders in my memory.

Afterwards, I asked Father Leveridge if I might have a word.

I told him about my Pernkopf volumes, their tainted history. What ethical issues were raised, did he think?

He was quiet for a time, looking into the distance.

'I think you want to keep these books. Otherwise you would have disposed of them already. So, the question for you is how to use them and keep your conscience clear.' A pause. 'There is no good answer. The origins of these books *are* despicable. But that cannot be undone. So, can they be used to help your patients? You are the one qualified to answer that, not me.' He turned to look at me directly. 'What I would say, is that whatever you decide should not be for you alone. What would your colleagues say? What would your patients say? They should be part of the decision-making.'

He saw right through me of course. That what I wanted was vindication of a decision already made. And *he* wasn't playing along.

What *would* my colleagues say? My fellow surgeons would be sympathetic, I think. But what about the anaesthetists or the theatre nurses or my constantly rotating junior staff? How much consultation would ever be enough?

As for the patients? If a look at Pernkopf's atlas could make it clear how to ease complex neurological symptoms, how many would say, *I'd rather you didn't?* And even if they did, how could I justify such inaction to myself?

So, Pernkopf sits as he did. At the back of my locker. In those rare instances when I feel the need to consult him, I do so surreptitiously. But then I find I want to linger. These paintings are masterpieces, after all. Even if tainted. And once you catch yourself, gazing at the whole painting rather than seeking the specifics of a solution, you have to wonder. Does tainted art also taint the viewer? Maybe. A work of art, if it is to touch us, needs its story to be known. Which is why perhaps, more than any other of Pernkopf's anatomical plates, I so often gaze on the painting of the dorsum of the hand.

Wendy Miller

SKIMMIN STANES WI MA WEE BRITHER

geed up tryin ah says, whitz the point
o these mark-missin dayz? wur aw scunnert.
But then you says tay me Backspin. Frisbee.
N ah felt a strange sense o epiphany
Loch Doon turnt roon n winkt at me
your words drappt like beats intay this treacle sea
harsh deep or shalla sweet it flows richt thru us baith.

So ah picked oot the best kinni stane
wee, oval n flat, fit fur the croassin, ken
ye showed me hoo tay lean in nice n low
(level wi a loach but staun up tay a sea)
by this time, ma stane wiz perched in the porch
atween thumb n forefingur
Don't Overthink It, ye sayz
Backspin. Flick. N lit go

when ah lit go ah felt aw ma failures take aff
fay ma fingurtipz fur the first time
ah'd harbuurt thum fur years
inside fists o fear. Well-nae-mare.
We baith stood back n held oor breath
watched as ah struck stane gold, conductin
four brass-bold skims, (doot doot doo doo)
n then. A fifth wan landit oan your lips
settlet intay a smile that could launch ships

ah did it

    ah did it

ah did it

    ah did it

AH DID IT

Marion F. Morrison

MO CHUIMHNE-SA AIR ASTRÀILIA

B' e sin taigh-beag, gun doras.
'Dunnie' mar a chanas iad
Air an achadh a-muigh
Iarann lurcach air a mhullach
Daolagan sa bhobhla
Ceud slat bho sheòmar-cadail
Luchd-obrach na rainse.

Tha mi beachdachadh air an seo
Nuair tha an currac dearg
Gar cuartachadh
Aig ciaradh an là
A' ruith air mo chorra-biod
Gus nach teid m' ithe le dingo
Tha mi a' cluinntinn am boobook ciatach
Anns a' chraobh-bhìthich chnapach
Agus luath cheumannan a' dol tarsainn
Seachad air nìd na circe mallee
Air an làr.
Mo chridhe nam bheul
Sgreuch a' khookaburra.

Os mo chionn
Crois a' Chinne Deas
Mar sgàil-riochd mu choinneamh
Na gealaich bhuidhe
Còig bleideagan reòdhta
Nan pristealan air ùrlar Fhlaitheanais
A' losgadh an fhàsaich
A' briseadh mo chridhe.

THE BEST PICTURE OF AUSTRALIA

It was a toilet with no door
A 'dunnie' as they call it
In a field
Corrugated iron roof,
Beasties in the bowl
One hundred yards from the ranch-hand dorm
And after the red canopy brings the day to its end
I imagine after sunset a frantic dash
Let me not be eaten by a dingo.
I hear the sinister boobook in the gum tree
Gnarled and dry and almost dead.
Nimble footsteps scrunch across the malleefowl nest
My heart sucked to my mouth
The kookaburra's wild laughter

Above me
The Southern Cross transfixed above the yellow moon
Five icy snowflakes set against a burning desert.
A moment in time
A memory to assuage
The mysterious aching of my heart.

Tom Newlands
AT JACKIE'S

Fulton's granda was called Jackie. He lived not far from me, up on the estate near the edge of the golf course. I'd seen Jackie round the town, round the estate too, but we had never done more than nod and raise the eyebrows. I skipped double History one November morning so Fulton could take me up to see him, just for a wee hello, he says.

To me there seemed to be two types of granda. You had the decent, round-faced granda who was usually a bit of a bloater and had white hair and sometimes a neat-looking beard. This type of granda owned jumpers. He gave you cake and praise and was predictable and smelt fine and nothing awful could come from being around him.

Then there were other, more menacing grandas that you saw existing in bookies or in the doorways of flat-roofed pubs. They were crumpled-looking and spindly. They wore brown suit jackets and had stale white hair that was turning yellow. They would call you the nicknames meant for adult women, give you money and drink, press their chests right onto yours when they came in for a cuddle.

'If he says anything weird just smile and agree with it,' Fulton goes as we walked, preparing me for something that might happen in that way he loved to do.

'Like, what's he going to say?' I goes. We turned onto the path behind the estate. The golf course was minty with frost.

'I dunno, but he's an old man. Just smile, like. Don't say anything stupid. Just go with it, Cora.'

We turned onto his street in our parkas. 'What do I call him?' I goes, seeing my breath.

'Jackie.'

'What do you call him?'

'Jackie,' he went.

'Alright, Jackie.'

Fulton stepped up and knocked. He shrugged once, took the hood down, his back went straight. His hair was the colour of cheddar cheese in the sun.

Jackie answered the door. Fulton goes, 'Hi Jackie.'

'Hiya Jackie,' I went, in my confidence voice. I could tell right away that he wasn't a granda that smelt like tumble driers or toffee.

Jackie said hello to Fulton without looking my way then wandered stiffly back into the house. Fulton gave me an earnest nod and I followed him into the dimness.

Jackie's hair was glossy and yellow like Stork. He had it slicked back down his neck like an American singer and from behind you could see where the different prongs of the comb had gone through the hair. He wore a vest with a low neck that left a puff of sparkly white chest hair sticking out like the blowball off a dandelion. He was the thinnest old man I had ever seen.

In the living room there were three armchairs and a low wood table made with brown ceramic tiles, arranged around a three-bar fire with dusty plastic coal in it. No TV, no carpet. The walls had been stripped down badly and there were shapes of differently-aged wallpapers left there, like in a crime scene on telly.

I was clamping my jaw to stop the chatters. We all sat down. Jackie had a right torn face like he was being freshly annoyed by some wee thing he thought he had already dealt with.

'Before I forget,' Fulton went, bringing a wad out of his coat pocket and counting notes into his granda's hands. I tried not to count along but it was over two hundred and twenty. Jackie didn't say thank you or acknowledge the money, he just flipped it in half round his purple thumb and pocketed it.

They started talking about football scores and games that had happened. Aberdeen had just done something in the league which was causing them concern. So-and-so was a cunt and a cheat. I thought, are old men – even the tramp ones – not supposed to have cardigans? He must be freezing. I tensed my arse-muscles in sequence on the seat as a way of releasing my nerves.

There were curtains. A butterfly-pattern lampshade round the bulb in the middle of the ceiling. Jesus being eerie on an old framed print. In the corner by the window was a crumpled pile of brownish clothes. Along the back wall by the door to the kitchen someone had arranged a load of golf clubs against the wall, individually spaced.

I knew that Fulton loved his granda but it was really hard to dream up any nice thoughts about the person who lived in this house.

Then Jackie stood up quickly, 'Do yous pair want a couple a cans?'

'Aye please, Jackie,' Fulton says. Hearing him call his granda by his first name was already setting me off.

While Jackie was in the kitchen Fulton turned to me and gave me a single serious nod. It said, *well done, thanks, I'm proud, I'm sorry*. I could tell he was on edge.

When Fulton wasn't out on the pavements at midnight head-locking his pals and setting fire to grit bins he was a gentler boy who got stressed quite easy about the things he really cared about. I saw that boy from time to time and thought about him quite a lot.

Jackie came bowling back with three cans of Sweetheart Stout, happier. There was a right-away feeling, a queasy-seeming feeling, at the thought of having to drink it. Two percent – puddle-water.

Jackie handed me mine without meeting my eye. We opened our cans at almost the same time with three flat, hollow clicks. It must have been about eleven A.M.

'So this is the bird, Fulton? Well done son.' Jackie went, sucking the foam out of the tin. They drank the same way, tilting the can up at their lips with one pinkie in the air while slurping. I took a sip. It tasted like the glue off an envelope.

Jackie looked at me and smiled, 'You're a wee stunner.'

'Aye, this is Cora.' Fulton looked at me expectantly.

'A right wee cracker,' Jackie said.

I smiled, 'Aw thanks. And thanks for the drink.'

'Cora's leaving school soon,' Fulton said. I kept the grin on like I was aware of this.

'Is she? Brilliant.' Jackie said. 'Are yous hungry at all? Can I heat yous up a pie?'

'No Jackie, thanks, we've had some sausage rolls on the way up.'

Jackie went to say something else but it was caught in a burst of sneezes, five or six of them. I was still smiling at the lie about the sausage rolls. Jackie wiped his nose then goes, 'So did I tell you son, I might be moving to Barrhead?'

'No, you never mentioned it.'

'Aye, I'm waiting to hear back from the council about a swap. Barrhead is a cracking wee place, like.'

All I knew about Barrhead was that it was miles away.

He went on, 'There's a flat there for me on the main street. Just a wee place up on the third floor, it would do me fine. And it's near the train station!'

'You'll miss the town though, eh?' Fulton said.

'Ach, to be honest son there's nothing for me here. All the boys I've worked with are dead. I've had my time here, like' Jackie went.

Fulton tried to do his grown-up nod.

I spoke up, 'Do you know people in Barrhead?' I took a sip to show I was enjoying it.

'Ach no,' he went. 'I know a few folk in Glasgow. Paisley. I'll be fine. Fulton will tell you, I live on my wits. I'll no have far to go to find some new pals. Isn't that right son?'

'Aye that's true!' Fulton said, grinning. I could tell he was surprised by all this, maybe even wounded.

'But listen, son. Don't you be worrying about it, it's way in the future. And you'll still be able to see me. Come and visit, bring your bird.'

Fulton said, 'Aye that would be amazing, Jackie.'

'There'll be a spare room, I've made sure of that. The council won't be moving me anywhere that I can't have my family over to! And there'll be a bed waiting for you, like. A double. And a fridge with plenty of drink.'

He cracked a huge smile that reminded me of his grandson. I took another tiny sip. I was beginning to notice the smell of the room. Most houses, even if they smelt bad, smelt of something that you knew – dogs, sweat, fags. Jackie's living room smelt of some sort of unknown vinegary chemical.

'Do you still have your budgie, Jackie?' Fulton asked, trying to keep everything going.

'He flew away, the wee cunt!'

'How did that happen then?'

'What do you mean how did it happen? He flapped his wings and fucked off. I had the windae open one day and he flew out. Never a problem before, I've always got my back door and my windaes open. Then one day he just flies off. Who knows what was going on in that wee pishy-coloured heid of his? I'll tell you one thing though – he'll no find seed like the seed I gave him. Deluxe Aviary Mix. Spoilt him rotten, the wee toerag. I gave him a broken up Wispa just the morning before he disappeared.'

'That must be so upsetting,' I said.

'That's no even the worst part,' Jackie said, louder now. 'The cunt flew across the road and sat on the roof of the newsagents over there, taunting me.'

'No way,' I went, turning to look out the window so I could hide my gulped-down chuckle.

'Aye! Every day for three weeks he was perched over there looking at me from across the road. I went over and shouted on him, stood in the garden trying to coax him over with some Pringles. And then when he'd had his fun he fucked off. Smug wee preening cunt!'

Jackie looked down, still shocked. I did a gentle smile to Fulton. I wondered how you could tell if a budgie was being smug or not.

They talked about the closure of Fusco's chippy. About a man called Rollo that Jackie bought homemade wine from. About different types of aftershave they liked. I sat with my legs crossed fiddling with the ring pull on my can, seeing in reality for the first time how Fulton hung on his granda's every word.

Then, 'Anyway,' Jackie goes suddenly, sitting up straight, 'Let's hear a wee bit about you, lassie.'

'What do you want to know?' I took a sip.

'So you're on Weavers Road? Gunner's lassie, that right?'

'Yeah,' I said, trying to make natural wee face movements.

'But this Gunner, he's no your real da?'

'No.'

'It's complicated,' Fulton said, making things worse.

'No it's not really that complicated. Basically, Jackie, I grew up just me and my mam. She had a few different boyfriends over the years,' I went.

'Nothing wrong with that,' Jackie said.

'Aye. My mam is gone now, she died. It's just me and Gunner.' My mouth was so dry. I took another drink. 'It's a bit of a weird one, but me and Gunner have always got on,' I went, hoping that would be enough.

'And so did he agree to being your da, no issues there?' Jackie said.

Fulton shunted himself awkwardly in his seat, chewing the skin round his thumbnail. I was praying he would keep quiet.

'Aye, well, he's not my da, but I think he likes me.' I did a single pathetic chuckle.

'And you live with this fella now, just you and him?' Jackie went.

'Aye. I'm an only child. His only child, I suppose?' I was unsure of it even myself.

'He sounds like a good fella, this Gunner.'

I chugged the rest of my stout and felt my tummy clench then clench again. A dash of boak came up. I felt guilty about tasting sick when Gunner was being discussed because none of it was as weird as it seemed.

'Aye, he's a good fella,' I went.

Then Jackie goes, 'So why do they call him Gunner?'

I put the can down. I thought of the real story then went, 'I don't know actually.' It was an easy enough thing to say. 'Michael McCallum is his real name.'

'Right. And you and this McCallum, you came from Muircross, Fulton tells me?'

'Aye, I grew up in Muircross.'

Jackie's face broke into a huge warm grin, 'A daughter of the Cross! You must be a right hard bitch, eh? Oh you poor wee thing. Listen, you made it out alive and that's the important thing, eh?'

'Muircross isn't the worst!' I went, cheery-like, wondering how you could be a hard bitch while crying so much in private.

'Aye it is,' he was laughing now. 'Aye it is! I had a pal in Muircross in the seventies, Peter Ranyard, good lad. Owned a camper van. Spent a wee bit of time there with him on a few odd jobs. It was an alright place then, a clean place with honest folk. Listen, I'm no trying to run down your wee hometown, but the only reason you'd go to Muircross now is for the eccies.'

'Right,' I went.

'Gunner no tell you any of this?'

'Not really, no.'

'Well anyway, you and Fulton make a nice couple. He'll take care of you. Just don't ever go back to Muircross!' I was about to reply when Jackie directed himself at Fulton, 'Listen son, before I forget,' he stood up, 'the pair of yous come through to the kitchen til I show you something.'

'Actually I need to go to the loo,' I went.

'Aye no problem lass, it's straight ahead of you once you're up the stair.' He pointed a milky arm at the ceiling then shuffled off toward the kitchen, Fulton in tow.

It was colder upstairs than it had been in the living room. I did the loo, keeping my arse up off the icy seat, wiggling myself due to the lack of paper. Jackie had a peach-coloured shower curtain with cartoon clouds on. After running my hands under the tap and drying them on my skirt I moved carefully across the bare floor of the hallway and had a look in the end bedroom.

The wallpaper was for kids and there was a dartboard on the far wall. The floor was covered in newspapers and in the middle there was a weightlifting bench. Some loose weights and empty cans and Woodpecker bottles were lined up in the corner. There was a single deformed Reebok on the windowsill. A tree outside was growing right up against the window blocking out most of the natural light.

Just as I turned away there was a noise from the other room. Male. A kind of suffocated grunt. Softly as I could, lead by my own nosiness, and with bravery suddenly appearing, I took a step towards the doorway and peeked my head around the open door for a look.

It smelt more sour in there. In the corner you saw an empty fish tank with a load of tubing in it, sat on a bin bag. Peering round further you saw a double bed, brand-new looking, with a velvety peach-coloured headboard. There were no covers or pillows on the bed, no table or chairs or anything you might find in a normal bedroom. And there on the bare mattress two men about Jackie's age were out for the count, grumbling and wheezing in separate sleeping bags. You could see their breath.

I froze myself in the doorway for a wee minute trying to come up with some lighthearted thoughts, then gave up and went back downstairs, doing the careful creeping steps so the stout still inside me wouldn't lurch around too much.

In the kitchen Jackie and Fulton were sat at a wooden table. The air smelt like old burgers. Between them they had a bottle of watermelon schnapps and a black nylon satchel, like a laptop bag.

'Here she is!' Jackie goes.

'Take a swally,' Fulton says, pointing the schnapps at me.

'I better not,' I went, and stayed standing with my hands in the breast pockets of my parka, showing it was time to leave.

Fulton took a too-long swig from the schnapps. Jackie seemed fine. There was no feeling from him that something unusual might be happening upstairs, or that I might have seen it. The clock on the cooker blinked with four red zeros.

After ten minutes of drink and chat Fulton got up and took the nylon bag and we said goodbye then left via the back door. I nodded and smiled and did the eyebrows then wedged myself halfway out the door behind Fulton to avoid any grope.

'What's in that bag?' I whispered as we waded through the long crispy grass.

'Pornos,' Fulton goes. 'Rare ones.' I fiddled with the latch on the tall wooden gate and we exited out onto the path. I shielded my eyes. The wee November sun looked like a pickled onion. I waited until he scraped the gate closed before replying.

'Why is your granda giving you pornos? That's so weird, Fulton.'

'It's not weird, he's finished with them,' he said.

We stood and looked at each other.

'Did you know your granda has people asleep upstairs in one of the rooms?'

'Aye, so? He lets people use his house. His mates. People come over and drink. It's a big house.' He started walking in the wrong direction.

'Where are we going?' I went.

'The golf course.'

We climbed the wall and walked together straight out into the middle of the deserted course, doing brittle-sounding footsteps in the minty grass. The satchel full of magazines bounced all flat and heavy on his hip.

He explained to me how the pornos were money in the bank because he could sell them round the schools. He told me he would hide them now and come back in future when he needed them.

He couldn't take them home because of fear of his da finding them. I wasn't sure if he meant that his da would punish him, or that his da would take them and sell them himself. Or that his da would use them himself.

I wanted to talk about Jackie going to Barrhead but he was moody-seeming and probably also wasted now, with the schnapps. We reached an island of bushes and trees in the middle of the course, not far from the clubhouse. There was a clearing where the long grass and weeds had been tramped down into a path and Fulton led me through the frozen gorse and into the undergrowth.

The clearing inside smelt of piss and ash. There were bottles and bin bags scattered about and a half-burned pallet with carpet underlay on it.

'Hold this,' Fulton went, and passed me the satchel of pornos. He got down on one knee and began to tuck his trackie bottoms into his socks. The wind in the bushes was hissing like telly fuzz. I guessed it wasn't even lunchtime yet.

'What are you doing?'

'I'm putting them up the tree where no cunt will find them,' he went, all natural.

'Can I help?'

'Lassies can't climb, Cora.' He started redoing his laces. Nosiness made me lift the flap on the bag and you saw in there the spines of twenty or thirty buckled-looking magazines. You could make out the different peach and plum-colour shades of nudieness.

'You upset Jackie's going to Barrhead?' I went.

'No, he's lucky. He's getting out of here,' he said, tugging his laces tight.

It seemed colder in the shelter of the bushes than it did outside. I looked up at the branches moving in the wind and wondered what else might be planked up there. My face hurt. I wanted to go home and eat heels of bread with soup then get Pauline round and sit on my covers with her watching Ren and Stimpy.

'There's nothing wrong with here,' I went.

'Weak talk, Cora.'

He sprang to his feet and did a little hop to ready himself for the challenge. His big round face looked damp and drunk and angry.

'Right,' he said and I handed him the satchel. He put the strap round his neck so the bag hung down his back. It was cutting right into his throat. 'You stay there and I'll be back down in a minute, then we'll go and grab more booze, eh?'

He leapt at the trunk and in three rapid moves was already well off the ground. Clumps of the tree shivered and shook as he moved. You couldn't help but be a wee bit impressed. As I looked up needles and twigs and little brown bits of tree-crap dropped down out of the branches and into my face and hair.

Catherine Ogston
THE OWL, THE CAT AND ME

'There is a baby owl living under our wardrobe,' I told my class.

Anticipation descended as an array of faces looked at me and then our teacher. Mrs Strachan favoured a blank expression, just sucking in her cheeks slightly.

'In the spare room,' I added.

Robbie Telford and his pals tittered at the back of the room while I stared right at our teacher, waiting for questions, admiration, intrigue.

But Mrs Strachan only looked at me, cleared her throat and announced, 'No, Rebecca. Owls don't live in houses. They live in woodlands, and trees and perhaps barns. Definitely not in wardrobes.'

'Under the wardrobe,' I said. 'Not in it,' as if that would be ridiculous. Everyone knows owls can't open doors.

Mrs Strachan used the same look on her face as the one Mum has when she is trying to stave off a headache.

'We have to keep the spare room door shut, of course,' I added. 'To keep Mr Beano out.'

'Mr Beano?' said Mrs Strachan, keeping her eyes blank and face straight and looking like she didn't want to know the answer.

'He's our cat,' I said. 'He would be very interested in the baby owl, for all the wrong reasons.'

That was the way Mum had explained it to Hannah and me, and I had liked the sound of it so I figured that was the best sentence to sum up why the owl and the cat couldn't be in the same room. Not like in that stupid poem about a pea-green boat.

'And how does the owl get food, living under your wardrobe?' said Mrs Strachan and I heard Robbie Telford do a pretend cough and stage-muttering a loud, 'McDonalds,' at the same time.

'The parents tap on the window and we let them in. We sit on the bed very quietly and watch them feed the baby owl. It's an owlet actually,' I said. Mrs Strachan pursed her lips and I knew I had gone too far. Adults always hate it when you know stuff they think you don't know.

'Fascinating,' said Mrs Strachan with her face not looking fascinated. It was looking like she was counting down the minutes until lunchtime.

'Miss!' bellowed Robbie, 'I have a crocodile under my bed. I do! It eats my homework!'

Mrs Strachan turned back towards her desk but I saw her roll her eyes so hard it must have hurt.

I searched out Lily Macleod and caught her eye. She stared back at me and then turned her gaze down to her desk. Disappointment pinched at me. She knew about the owlet and she knew about Uncle George. But now she acted like I had made both things up.

'I could bring in a photo,' I said, my voice sounding whiny. Desperation leaked from me like a hose with punctures. Watching that baby owl every night was the only nice thing in my life and no one even believed it was real.

'Okay Rebecca, you do that,' said Mrs Strachan in a tight voice, like she thought there was no chance this would ever happen. Perhaps she was thinking about how many days until the end of term and how many days of freedom she would have until she had to start again with thirty new faces in front of her, a new Robbie Telford playing the class clown and a new Rebecca Davies with tall tales.

No one would use that look on me if I had proof. Tonight I would get my phone and and sit quietly with Hannah on the spare room bed, ready to press 'record'. I would wait until the tapping at the window started and then I would use my thumb on the red button and film the owl parents edging forward on the open windowsill. I would train the camera on them flying into the room and depositing food for the fluffy owlet which lived under the wardrobe ever since the day they flew down the chimney. We would sit like statues until the parents left and we had pushed the window shut and the owlet had shuffled under the wardrobe again. And then, like every evening, I would say to Hannah the same message I always told her. Don't be alone with Uncle George. Ever. Promise me.

She was only six. But she was old enough to know that I meant it.

'Okay Becca,' she had said to me last night, like she did every night. 'But I like Uncle George.'

Of course she did. He made her laugh, brought us sweets and DVDs, offered to babysit us when Mum went to visit Dad in hospital. 'He's just pretending to be nice,' I had told her and she looked at me like I was crazy. She looked at me the same way Mrs Strachan looked when I told her there was an owl under the wardrobe. I shook her by the shoulders.

'This is important,' I had told her. 'Do you want the baby owl to die?'

I don't know why I said that but her face crumpled.

'No!' she wailed, her bottom lip wobbling.

'Well, remember what I am telling you,' I said. I let go of her shoulders and she sprang away from me, jumping down from the bed and running out the door, leaving it ajar. A few seconds later Mr Beano's grey stripy face poked itself eagerly around the open doorway and I shooed him out, shutting the door firmly behind me.

Owlet under the wardrobe.

Mr Beano on the prowl.

Dad hooked up to beeping machines and a tube in his throat.

Uncle George, wearing a mask of niceness.

Lily Macleod knowing my darkest secret and making me wish I could go back and never ever tell it to her.

'Rebecca,' Mrs Strachan was saying, 'did you hear me?'

'No, Miss, I was talking to the tarantula in my schoolbag,' warbled Robbie in a high-pitched voice which sounded nothing like me.

I blinked at her.

'I said, I would like a word, after the bell?'

I nodded, and sat there for the next hour with my heart racing. Surely this was the day that Lily had told someone, who had told someone else, and now I was never going back home, and Mum would cry even more and Hannah would be more alone than ever and that owlet was going to be toast.

*

'Rebecca,' said Mrs Strachan, 'I know things are difficult at home just now. But making up lies is not a good choice.'

Teachers love talking about choices.

Sweat was making the backs of my knees itchy and I leaned over to scratch one while I waited to hear which lie I had told.

'There's not an owl under your wardrobe, is there?' said Mrs Strachan and I looked hard at her face. There was an orange line around her jaw and a crusted spot on her chin which she had smeared a beige splodge of concealer onto. Her morning lipstick had faded, half of it smudged onto her travel mug that she carried about like it had a life-sustaining potion in it.

'Well, there is, and you can believe it or not, I guess,' I said because suddenly it didn't feel like my job to convince her. Mrs Strachan's mouth dropped open as she did a quick calculation of how many rules of school behaviour I had just broken. It flapped open and shut and open again and then disappeared into a thin line.

A sudden thump on the window made us both jump and Mrs Strachan's mouth transformed itself back to normal, an unhappy squiggle on her face. Robbie Telford's coupon appeared, framed by a glass pane, all freckles and grins, shouting, 'Sorry Miss, my ball went squint.' Mrs Strachan sighed and went back to staring at me. Robbie stayed at the window pulling faces behind her back, then disappeared with his hand clutched at his neck like he was being hauled away on an invisible rope. I felt a sudden affection for him. Nothing life-changing. A seven out of ten for consistency if nothing else.

'While I have you here,' she announced, rummaging on her desk for a piece of paper, her voice softening slightly, 'there was a message for you. You've to go straight to the hospital after school today.'

'Me and Hannah?'

'No, just you I think. Hannah is being picked up by your uncle, after Craft Club.'

And right then I felt all the lines of my life converging onto one point.

*

The owlet took its time to venture out from the wardrobe. It was most likely confused by the lack of a mouse dinner and the absence of its parents. There was only me, sitting in the corner of the room while Mr Beano did scritchy-scratchy scrabbles with his paws on the other side of the closed spare room door. Cold wind blew in from the open window which I didn't mind because I had done a muscles-burning, lungs-wheezing run all the way home. I had run right past the hospital and didn't think about Dad lying there with bleeps and whirrs and a pump puffing up and down like a concertina and Mum there too, red-eyed and exhausted.

My phone was in my hand, ready to hit the record button, when it vibrated.

Lily's name appeared on my screen and my heart jolted.

You should definitely film the owl, it said.

I stared. A second message arrived.

I know you are not lying.

I didn't have any time to process this; Lily reappearing in my life after listening to my secret and yet making it feel twice as heavy and razor-edged. Just then the owlet poked his face out from beneath the gap under the wardrobe and surveyed the room, gliding its head to and fro softly under his new feathers. He eyed the patch of blue open sky and shuffled towards it, scattering white downy feathers until they flew around him like swirling snowflakes. He stretched and fluttered his wings and twitched his head, like he was weighing up a decision. I pressed 'record' and watch him flap, fly, falter and try again until he was perched on the windowsill. I would like to say he swivelled his head round and gave me a long last glance but he had his mind on all the world before him, not behind. He launched himself out of the window, uttering a call to his parents as he went. Perhaps it said, *I'm here, find me*, or *I'm hungry*. Or perhaps it said, *I'm fed up living under a wardrobe, squashed and lonely.*

After he had gone I hung out the window staring towards the sky, and staring down the street. By then I had opened the door and let Mr Beano in. He did a lot of investigatory sniffing and patrolling before jumping up and joining me at the open sill, peering out into the great beyond, most likely wondering if he should launch himself into mid-air to find his missing owl dinner.

I was waiting for Hannah and Uncle George. I would see his car, and watch them walk through the front door before tearing down the stairs, and grabbing Hannah's hand and pulling her with me back out onto the street. We would run and as we turned the corner of the road I would glance back to see Uncle George standing there, his face a thundercloud, his mask slipping.

Tonight I would tell Mum my secret because it had been sitting inside me for too long. And then I would be able to fly free, just like that baby owl, my worries falling like unwanted feathers to the ground.

Lauren Pope
THE TIMES I DIDN'T USE MY NAME

When I was the [   ] between two sounds, a thought in their
heads, a penny oxidising at the bottom of the well, the fabric of
becoming   before the simplest

                                        linguistic act,

before I howled
         me   and felt the warm wind, the buoyancy of it,

                                being raised like a flag.

                            *

Strange elocution: picture yourself as a question in the mouths
         of others.
                            That's how it was –
the elongated year I learned that staring is the truest expression
                                            of interest,

             People asked questions –
                    Where do you live?
                            Why aren't you in school? –
             the way a hammock rocks

             against its chain.

             Chloe was a decoy, a name I borrowed
                from Fashion Star Fillies. Believe me,

             I was equine.

                            *

Ferns burst arrogantly
    from impossible places;

   on my CV, the words *extrovert* and *people-person.*

   My true affinity lies with the poppies –
  rows of anaemic sisters
    bruising under the scrutiny –

   thoughts of *procrastination*

   buried beneath the dirt.

      *

Some things are sewn into life with the thinnest of thread.
   The colour of it –
pale pink/ blue – is not the important thing here.

On the sign-in sheet at Planned Parenthood:
   You don't expect to be here when your 40
   C'mon Barbie/ Jenny from the Block/ Bonita Applebum
   Pulling out method
   Young & dumb

   My second visit I wrote *VOID*, in all caps,

      like it was a request.

      *

I was thinking about my walls, I was thinking
         about the yellow cliffs   eroding
                  along the coastline;
         if I am to be named one thing,
                  let it be that

& then a woman hollered at me from the opposite side

         of the road. We were friends in TZ, many years back.
I didn't respond, kept walking, but it was quite something to be
         reminded
                                                    of that life
         like stepping into old shoes – both mine, and not;
                  a newly minted snake forced into its discarded skin.

Allan Radcliffe
BAIRNS

Tat-tat-tat on the other side of the wall. *Tat-tat-tat-tat-tat*. When eventually I've disentangled myself from the blankets and cushions and made my way through the house, the hammering has ceased and my brother is kneeling in a circle of cardboard and ripped-open plastic bags. The frame of a child's bed gleams out of the debris.

'Come see.'

He places a hand on the box spring and leans against it, nodding over my shoulder. I confront a lime-green wall and a yellow wooden clock that's floating between carpet and ceiling. It's like being dunked inside a cartoon.

'When are you expecting her?'

'Saturday, all being well.' He passes a hand in an agitated way over his head. 'You'll still be here on Saturday? Okay. Good. She'll want to see you.'

He shoots another look at the feature wall.

'Think she'll like all this? The bairn?'

We face the sunflower clock, our heads on the side. Rebecca's almost nine now. When I think of her, I see a child of four, clarty from playing out with her friends, the little group piling through the back door at Niall and Claire's house in Queensferry. A solemn wee face: when she smiled you knew she meant it.

'Are you absolutely sure she likes green?'

His mouth twitches and his body begins to tremble, lightly at first and then almost violently, all his pent-upness shuddering out. Afterwards he wipes his eyes, coughs and looks away from me, mortified at his lack of restraint.

'Aye, she likes green. So I'm told.'

*

Niall suggests a bite at the new place on the corner of Bernard Street. We step out into a monochrome day. Since splitting up with

Claire, my brother has been staying in a flat near the shore, about as far north as you can get without ending up in the Forth. Every available edifice here has been remade from the inside out so the disposable-income brigade can enjoy a glimpse of the Fife coastline with their muesli.

We perch on swivel stools and order the full Scottish. The waiter brings a pot of coffee and juice in jam jars with straws. I watch my brother fish out the stripy tube and break the surface of his drink with his lips, making a face like it's good for him.

'How long's it been, Niall?'

'Six months, near enough.'

'This is the longest . . .?'

He shrugs.

'You're doing well on it. I mean: you've got a bit of colour in your cheeks.'

He signals the waiter, waving his jar. 'More of this . . . *stuff*, please.'

*

Niall and Jordan. Our teachers had field days. *Did your mum and dad have a thing about rivers?* The truth was less poetic. Niall was named after a friend of our father's from his roaring days. Mum had her heart set on Jordan for me: boy or girl. They didn't clock what they'd done until it was too late. Dad thought the whole thing hilarious. Mum worried folk would think they were hippies.

Because Niall was five years older than me he got to do everything first. From the age of fifteen he was allowed to work in the shop two evenings a week and nine-to-six on Saturdays. The scene at cashing up time was always the same: Niall on his knees in front of the crisp wall, Walkman wires trickling down the side of his face. Mum, bird-eyed with a pen behind her ear, thumbing through the leftover papers, and Dad at the end of the counter, eviscerating the puzzles section of the *Herald*.

The counter area was separated from the back shop and the flat upstairs by a beaded curtain that brattled as the strings of wood and bamboo lifted and dropped back into place. Dad would shout 'Jordy!' as soon as he heard the beads clicking, and he would pull me into the armpit of the dark jacket he always wore, the one Mum kept holding up and saying had seen better days.

I breathed in his cake mixture smell until he held me further and further away from him, loosening his grip, 'Ah'm gonnae drop ye!' Blue eyes cut in half by drooped lids – also Niall's eyes, my eyes. My brother scowled over at us. A year later he would graduate to the Wimpy on Princes Street where all the best-looking girls in his year worked.

*

I clung to the brightly lit shop. It was safe in the way the outside world with its baiting, soft-bearded boys was not. I'd sit through the back, scarfing crisps and reading my way through the tied stacks of magazines.

It was there, aged twelve, riffling through some old mags on the desk where my parents kept their paperwork that I found my first copy of For Women and fell in love with Todd, that month's full-frontal centrefold.

With his rigid hair and ludicrously square jaw, Todd looked like a cartoon hero – Fred from Scooby Doo or a Disney prince – only with glossy pubes, a sponge-like scrotum and a belly that seemed to go on forever.

The soft focus lent the image a dreamlike quality. Everything about him – his skin, his hair and his eyes – shone. I tore Todd from the magazine, folded him at the belly button and tucked him away in my bag, my heart hammering. I wore the page ragged, folding and unfolding until beautiful Todd ghosted away to nothing.

Before Todd, I read the Beano, Look-In, Smash Hits, books about kids who solved crimes. Mum read Nursing Times and the Sunday supplements. Niall liked the football magazines, his Hibs souvenir programmes and the back half of the Record. Dad loved crossword puzzles, word searches and quizzes. When he was concentrating he used to let his mouth hang open while he stroked his jawline. His pals were always telling him he should apply for *Fifteen-to-One*. 'Naw, that's not for me,' he would say, 'I'm not one for being the centre of attention,' and, spooked at the very thought, he would reach for the nearest available container of drinkable liquid.

*

Niall lifts his jam jar. 'Anyway, so here's to you. Been a while.'

'You'll need to come and visit. You and Rebecca.'

'Long time since I was in London.'

'In the new year, then, once you're in a routine with her.'

'That's a done deal.'

In the past two decades I've lived in Spain, France, the Czech Republic and London. My brother hasn't visited me in any of them. I wouldn't even bet on him owning a passport.

When I phoned and told him I was thinking of coming home for a few days he asked if something was the matter.

'It's Reading Week,' I told him. 'I've got the time off.'

'You get a week off to read?'

'It's for the students. Skiing Week, we call it.'

'Nothing's happened?'

'Do I need an excuse to see my one and only brother?'

I could hear his breath juddering on the line.

'Well,' he said, 'it's been – what – five years?'

The food arrives and we eat diligently. I blear out the window. The sun has come out with a sudden glorious heat. Everyone that goes past carries that look of wild relief that comes with a gap in the clouds.

Me, I feel like I'm sitting with an acquaintance: someone I can't curse or spill in front of. The tape machine on the counter is playing *One More Day* from *Les Mis* and I want to stand on my chair and warble along. Niall's hunched over his plate and he's pushing forkfuls into his mouth. I've always had to guess what my brother is thinking. There are times when I have to ask him open questions, the way I would the more challenging of my students, to elicit answers of more than one syllable. The devil in me wants to start telling him about my sex life just to see how he copes.

*

I can barely remember a time when Claire and Niall weren't together. They met in the Conan Doyle one Saturday when Claire was over to see a gig at the Playhouse. When they were first going out, they spent weekends in our flat. Claire's mum and dad were old school and wouldn't let Niall stay over, not even in the spare room.

Saturday nights, when they were skint, I'd sit with them while they watched *Blind Date*, *Casualty*, *Stars in their Eyes*. I liked Claire: she put up with me. *Wee bro*. Our chatter would drop off after a while and the place would fall silent save the rattle from the telly, and then all the nose-breathing from the other end of the couch would start up, and then it would intensify.

A feeling rose off that couch, something I couldn't name, collecting in the air and growing towards me. Just when I was getting ready to scuttle away, Niall and Claire would rise with contented sighs and edge towards the door – '*Night then, Jordan,*' – bound for the double mattress wedged between the walls of the box room. Not very private, but it was more comfortable than the Eastern Cemetery.

Niall and Claire. Claire and Niall. They seemed so much more than two people who shared a mortgage and a kid. They were old friends. I sometimes found them in corners, ending themselves at some mysterious joke.

*

Niall drops his fork. 'Well, if that was my lunch, I've had it.'

He reaches behind him and feels in his coat pocket, bringing out a pouch of tobacco and a packet of fag papers in a fluster of coins and paper hankies.

I watch him fumblingly fashion a rollup. Despite his years of imbibing he has never acquired a gut. His profile is as sharp at forty-seven as it was at twenty-four.

'I'll get the bill.'

His face becomes tense as he strains in his seat, attempting to signal the waiter, who's leaning over the counter, talking to another customer.

'God's sake, do his lips not get frayed . . .?'

He returns to his roll-up, letting his mouth hang open, tightening the paper around the tobacco with one hand while agitating his stubble with the other.

*

As time passed, Dad gave up his spot at the end of the counter and took to sitting on a stool under the fags display with the puzzle pages spread out on the floor. Shoplifters ran riot. Niall chased after them, his cheeks livid. Dad still stroked his jawline, but it had become a means of keeping himself awake between sittings at his local.

Our father knew many people and every one of Dad's friends had a smell you could taste. I lost track of the amount of free baccy my father gave away, the number of times I heard him say, 'Ocht, don't be daft,' when Tony or Gordon or Maxie delved into their trouser pockets and made a big show of rattling their change. These men would go through the rigmarole of objecting, rounding their mouths, admonishing Dad for being too generous for his own good, too good for this world.

Which of course he was. Profit meant nothing to him against the good opinion of his friends.

'Not one word to your mother,' he'd say if I happened to be there to witness one of his many acts of charity.

Once, when I was helping in the shop, because I was finally old enough and Dad had slowed, I tried taking money from a man named Adie Morrison, who I knew fine well hadn't paid

for his halves of Old Holborn since he lost his job as a gas fitter
in the late Eighties. As I held out my hand Dad sprang like
Zebedee from his berth behind the counter. Adie backed away,
returning his damp fiver to his pocket, baccy and papers tight in
his other fist.

'Won't. Tell. Mum,' I recited, slamming the till, turning to grab
up a two hundred pack of Lambert & Butler, tearing into the paper.
Dad blinked over at me a couple of times, disorientated at having
been forced to his feet so abruptly.

He no longer had the attention span for puzzle pages. He had
gone past the point of anything animating him any more, even the
sight of me at the end of a day. He spent most of his time dozing,
and when he was awake, his eyes were on things that were nothing
to do with the present.

*

Niall and I head back along the road, our breath stealing a march
on us. 'It's just so bastard dark already,' says Niall, with a kind of
awe in his voice. I try to make him laugh by attempting to avoid
the cracks in the pavement.

Up in the flat, my brother gives me a vague instruction to help
him straighten the place out while he lugs the hoover through to
Rebecca's bedroom. My case is dumped at one end of the couch,
the arm of my pink Reiss shirt lolling down the side. This is all I've
got with me, one measly bag, but when I had packed for the trip
my flat looked as bare as when I moved in.

*

London is defeating me. From the start the place seemed to close
in on me, the sky too far away. I have often been on my own but
I've never been lonely.

On my first day at the college, the head of the department
paraded me through the staffroom, clapping the other teachers
to attention.

A few muted hellos. I stood around the little beige cube, smiling at the edge of conversations I hadn't been invited to join.

That set the pattern. Elsewhere, everyone was an outsider, so people gravitated towards each other. Here, the other teachers were coupled-up or they were ten years younger than me with three times the stamina.

For a time I went with the younger ones to their pubs and, when pressed, told them the soda water I'd sneaked from the bar was gin-and-tonic. Elsewhere, sitting for hours nursing a juice was considered acceptable. Here, people lived for their Friday binge. I hadn't been around this much desperate drinking since my childhood.

*

I'm fine, I tell myself. I'm in *London*, for God's sake. Let the fun commence!

I take myself off to preview nights at the theatre. Sit in the gods, soaking up whatever bodily warmth the person in the next seat gives off. I take a trip to the National Gallery, ascend to the Impressionists and lose myself in row after row of coloured dots. I read everything I can lay my hands on: from dollar classics to thrillers people leave lying around the staffroom, or I bury myself in screens. I become addicted to certain porn sites, attaching to my favourite adult performers so completely that I begin to think of them as my friends.

I travel across town on the tube for hookups, marvelling at the wee nooks my dates can squeeze themselves into while they tell me, proudly, how much they're paying in rent.

I start thinking about my mother, Niall, Rebecca. For the first time in years I start wondering what it would be like to go home.

*

When I visited five years ago I arrived late from the airport to find Claire waiting but no Niall.

'Look, I've no idea when your brother's getting back. Shall we eat?'

We sat across from each other and talked about things from the past. She and Niall hardly went out these days, and Claire had taken to searching for their old friends on Facebook and listening to the music of her twenties on YouTube.

At some point we heard the front door rattle. Niall stood in front of us, his eyes searching and adjusting.

'Jordan?' His features made a dash for the centre of his face. 'You're winding me up. Did we say tonight?'

'I phoned a couple of times,' Claire said. 'I left messages.'

'Fuck, sorry mate.' Niall stumbled into the room. 'No idea what I've done with my mobile.' Claire's eyes never left Niall once. As she was lowering the lid back down onto the tajine, Niall poured himself a tumbler of water and knocked it back.

My brother walked towards me very slowly and deliberately. He plopped himself down and the smell of whatever he'd been drinking joined us at the table.

'The wee bro. What do you think, Claire?'

She was standing in the doorway. She was looking at Niall as though he reminded her of someone she couldn't quite place. She looked weary. Worse, she looked bored. She was bored of him, hungry for change, as though the only thing keeping her in that doorway and in that house was a huge effort of will.

Niall spun his head in either direction, trying to catch her up in his glance. He slumped to the side, his elbow just missing the chair-arm. At least in the dim kitchen light I didn't have to look closely. In a couple of days I'd be gone and then I wouldn't have to look any more.

*

Niall's poised at the headboard of Rebecca's bed. 'Into that corner,' he says, signalling with his head.

He grips the edge of the headboard. I believe he'd tidy me out the way if he could. We lift the bed on three. Niall pushes forward with such force that I stumble and let go my end.

'Jordan, you're feeble.'

'Hey. Remember our bunk beds?'

Niall winces. 'How did we manage to go all those years without killing each other?'

'That flat was a tip. Mum spent her life fixing things.'

'One sticking plaster after another holding the whole place together.'

'And the creaking loft. You told me there were ghosts.'

'Did not.'

'Covers up to the chin. Terrified.'

*

He was at times a good brother to have around. In the rammy of the playground he stayed close, helicoptering in when necessary. He put himself between me and the boys shouting *bufty*, just long enough for me to get away to the library. I spent the lunch breaks reading with my coat on. And when I had read my way through the single-shelf section marked Scottish Literature I realised how predictable our family was in many ways, how unsurprising its quiet, drinking men.

But I could never find myself in those crowded pages, and there were times when I had to run to a mirror to remind myself that I did in fact exist. Ah, there I was. Jordan Grieve. Boy. But not a Boy, at least, not in the way my brother was a Boy.

*

When my parents gave up the shop we moved into a flat on the fifth floor of an eight-storey Lego-brick block on the Southside. The development was so new that the clutter from the site hadn't been cleared away: it lay in heaps around the building.

All the baby-fat freshness was gone from my father. I couldn't watch any more. I went hunting for his stashes. I gathered his bottles together in a bag but then I just stood there, in the middle of the kitchen: my plan wasn't fully formed.

Niall, watching from a corner of the room, came to life.

'I know what to do.'

We stepped out into the landing. The rubbish chute was in one corner, behind a heavy swing door. It had fascinated us when we moved in: we scouted for things we could throw in it, the more fragile the better.

Niall and I squeezed through the door with the chinking bag. We took it in turns to push the bottles through the narrow opening. Niall drove them down the chute with such force it made me take a step away from him.

He was seventeen or eighteen then, in his last year at school. There was an edge to him, a kind of determination.

*

Niall downs tools around eight and we wander across to Ocean Terminal. He nods towards the closed-down shops and the twenty-four-hour gym: he works out there a couple of times a week, first thing before the office. He grins, bashfully flexing one arm. We eat noodles in Wagamama's then board the escalator to the multiplex. The only film starting within the hour is *The Last Witch Hunter*, which turns out to be a big special effects number with Vin Diesel and half a feature's worth of plot. We're restless, our hands colliding above the bag of Revels between our seats. We stifle our giggles with our sleeves. It's a feeling I barely remember from childhood, this shared inanity. Niall disappears and when he returns I can almost taste the second-hand smoke. He stretches out and closes his eyes. I start to wonder what we must look like to the folk around us, a pair of six-footers sliding around in our seats like the big bairns we are.

Tracey S. Rosenberg
THE WESTERN WALL

'It's my grandmother's number. They deported her to the Theresien-stadt ghetto when she was fifteen. Then she survived Auschwitz.' Susie stretched her muscular left arm over the top of the plastic chair. On her outer forearm was a ragged blue A followed by a hyphen and five numbers.

The tattoo practically shimmered in the heat. We were all so greased up with sunblock on our first day in Jerusalem, we might as well have been a collection of skinny plucked chickens in sunglasses, awaiting our turns in the fryer.

'I'm sorry,' I murmured, hoping Susie didn't hate me for asking. When I first saw her tattoo, I'd assumed it was some meaningless inspirational slogan like *breathe* or *exhale*.

Was I supposed to match Susie's grandmother with my own relative? Maybe it was a Jewish tradition to trade stories about Holocaust survivors. But my mother said all of her ancestors got the hell out of Russia at the turn of the twentieth century, and hightailed it straight to America, where they sold encyclopedias and put up Christmas trees and chopped the 'stein' off their name.

Nechama scowled at Susie. Her feet were tangled in the straps of her backpack. 'You didn't think that tattoo was the stupidest decision ever? Talk about internalising the oppressors.'

Susie rolled her eyes. 'It's not some airheaded tramp stamp. If people don't remember the past—'

'People don't remember *all* the past. I don't see any international days of mourning about the Zionist takeover of Palestine. But go ahead, keep playing the Shoah as the ultimate victim card.'

'I'm trying to write to God,' I snapped.

Susie and Nechama twisted away from each other.

In front of us rose the Western Wall. Maybe I was still too jet-lagged and dazed from the heat, but I wasn't feeling anything close to awe as I looked up at the remnants of the Second Temple.

It was as if I'd finally visited the Louvre, walked up to the Mona Lisa, and cried, 'Is that *it*?' But maybe that wasn't a fair comparison. Even Leonardo himself never claimed that God was present in the Mona Lisa, while a lot of people believed the wall itself was sacred.

I had to admit, the wall's mere existence was pretty impressive, given all the fighting around it over the course of two thousand years – though I only knew a few hazy facts about Byzantines and Crusaders and the British Mandate. The wall's lower layers were massive blocks of white and sandy stone, weathered and scored. On the upper span, green bushes sprouted like the beards of the black-hatted men I'd seen on our way through the Jewish quarter. I couldn't believe those bushes were allowed to grow. Wouldn't their roots spread through the stones and eventually crack the wall to pieces?

Along the wall's bottom hem, women rocked in prayer or pressed their foreheads against the stones. Women with every strand of hair bundled up in patterned scarves, women in glossy expensive wigs, schoolgirls with curly ponytails and ankle-length skirts. I could only see women, because a perpendicular barrier divided the base of the wall into two unequal parts. The men in our tour group had been shunted off, a few of them cupping their hands around the tops of their heads, worried they'd prompt an international incident if their unfamiliar kippas flew off.

Two men in high-viz vests moved around the women's section, stacking white plastic chairs no longer in use. Those chairs seemed almost sacrilegious for contemplating a holy relic, more appropriate for lazing on during a muggy summer day, eating a popsicle that dripped sugary trails down the side of your hand. Sometimes, as one of the men dragged a tower of chairs to the far edge of the plaza, they had to pause because a woman was shuffling backwards across their path. I thought the heat was playing games with my vision, but no – woman after woman retreated from the wall while still facing it.

'Do you *have* to leave the wall backwards?' I asked, but Susie was reading from a prayer book, her lips moving.

The crevices of the lower wall were stuffed with white flakes – paper missives as high as the arm could reach. 'You can write to God,' our group leader told us, before moving forward to join the mass of praying women. But my paper remained blank. I wished I had the nerve to peek at some of the papers already placed in the wall. Were they profound cries to the King of Kings, Blessed Be He? Or did people treat the wall like a celestial vending machine – prayers go in, gifts come out?

Susie closed her book. 'You can leave the wall however you want. Some people don't want to turn their backs on the Divine Presence.'

Nechama was glancing around, as if trying to sneer in all directions at once. 'So what did your grandmother say about your stupid tattoo?'

Susie gripped the prayer book as if she'd like to bash it over Nechama's head. 'First she screamed, and then she cried. She kept trying to hug me, but her oxygen tank was in the way, so it ended up being a lot of little pats. She told me she'd wanted twenty children, to make up for her lost family – everyone was murdered, except one of her younger brothers, but she didn't know he'd survived until after he was already dead. He thought *he* was the only one left, so after liberation, he joined the Haganah and fought in the War of Independence—'

'The Year of the Catastrophe.' Nechama looked ready to spit.

'That was 1948, right?' I asked quickly.

Susie nodded. 'In the end, she only had my mom, and my mom only had me. So I'm the one person from my family going into the future. I'm not always sure whether my grandmother is talking to me, or to her sister Zusanna who died in the ghetto. Sometimes I dream I *am* Zusanna.'

'She's your root,' I said.

Nechama bent down and scrabbled in her backpack, turning it as if making sure neither Susie nor I could see inside. I assumed it held the things listed on our pre-tour checklist – sunscreen, plug adapters, scarves to cover our shoulders when we visited sites that required women to behave modestly. I didn't learn what Nechama's backpack actually contained until months later, after her death made international headlines. Her grieving parents sued the state of Israel, claiming their daughter had been unlawfully killed. But the Supreme Court ruled that Nechama deliberately placed herself in a dangerous situation, and died in the framework of a war-related activity. 'She came to Israel on an international tour that encouraged young Jews of the diaspora to connect to their ancestral home,' an opinion piece in the *Jerusalem Post* claimed after the verdict. 'Yet this was merely a cover for her true intentions: to shield and, indeed, to facilitate terrorist activity.' Part of the court's decision was based on the contents of Nechama's backpack – she did have sunscreen and a scarf, but she'd also packed two burner phones, a chequered black-and-white keffiyeh, a GoPro, and three hundred fliers denouncing illegal Israeli settlements in Hebron.

Susie had replaced her prayer book in her own backpack. 'On Friday nights, before the start of Shabbat, IDF soldiers come here. They dance in circles, wearing their guns, and they sing.'

Nechama snapped her backpack shut. 'Do they also sing when they shoot unarmed protestors with live ammunition?'

Susie launched into 'Am Yisrael Chai'. The tune was simple and there were maybe six words endlessly repeated; our group leaders had taught us the song on the bus trip from Ben Gurion Airport.

We only had a few more minutes before we all had to make our way back to the main plaza, through the narrow markets where men implored us to buy souvenirs and spices, and to the Jaffa Gate to meet our bus. I still had no idea what to tell or ask God. I could barely write the Shema in English, much less Hebrew, a language of squiggles and dots. (Or was it Aramaic? I couldn't remember the difference.) But no doubt there were thousands of Shemas jammed into the wall, since it was the holiest prayer.

'Does your grandmother still believe in God?' I asked Susie. 'After everything she went through in the Holocaust, and all the people who died?'

'She never believed in God. She never even ate matza until she came to Brooklyn.' Susie stroked her tattoo. 'They were so assimilated in Vienna, she barely knew she was Jewish. Her father didn't think about emigrating because it was incomprehensible that anything would happen. By the time the Nazis forced him to scrub the streets with his toothbrush, it was too late.'

'But why did the Nazis care about people who weren't Jewish?'

'They *were* Jewish. It isn't what you do, it's who you are. Bloodlines go back and back.'

Nechama stood. 'Fucking Chosen People.' She hefted her backpack and marched away towards the main plaza, turning her back to the wall.

'Would the Nazis have come after *me*?' I asked. 'I'm only half-Jewish. I've never gone to a synagogue in my life, and most of what I know about Judaism is from Wikipedia. I only came on this trip because it was free.'

'There's your proof,' Susie said, with a wicked little laugh. 'Seriously, though, if your mother's Jewish, you are too. And you'd both have been crammed into the same cattle car as my grandmother.'

I wanted to splash ink all over my blank paper. 'It doesn't make sense that I count as fully Jewish even though it's only on one side. My father's family are all from Denmark, but no one ever argues I'm a hundred percent Danish.'

'You do look Scandinavian.' Susie scrutinised me. 'With your blonde hair – and, let's face it, that's not a Jewish nose – you could easily have been smuggled out and raised by a Christian family. But you're a member of the tribe even if you never eat a bite of matza. We should get going; the men are already back at the plaza.'

'Just let me write this letter.' I wished I were a kid again, when I spent hot days lounging in a chair and licking popsicles, instead of imagining my naked mother being shoved into a gas chamber.

*

Susie was the only person I kept in touch with from our tour group. A decade later, she phoned to congratulate me on the birth of my sixth child – Miriam Celia, named after two of my husband's great-aunts who had died at Majdanek. I was always glad to hear from Susie, both for her dose of Americana and her lack of judgment. My mother had been furious with me for years. At first it was because I abandoned my college degree and bought a one-way ticket to Tel Aviv. Then, after going to the Western Wall every Shabbat to watch the IDF soldiers dance in circles, I said hello to one of them in my faltering Hebrew, and married him three months later. After Yonatan left the army and we moved to Modi'in Illit, my mother started complaining there was no excuse for living in an illegal settlement – and how had I, raised in modern secular America, decided my life should include misogynist rituals such as not touching my husband when I was menstruating, and covering my hair with a scarf?

'I shaved my head,' I finally snapped. 'It's what women do in my community. It's more modest. I wear a wig, and when I go outside, I cover the wig with a scarf.'

My mother hadn't spoken to me since.

After Susie and I chatted for a while, me with one ear towards the room where my younger children were napping, I came back to a topic I'd been pondering for the previous decade. 'Nechama turning against her own religion so violently – is it too simplistic to call her a self-hating Jew?'

I expected Susie to launch into a stream of jargon. After all, she was about to complete her doctorate in sociology, researching the effects of early trauma on geriatric populations. But she only said,

'You should know better than any of us, there are no simple answers in Judaism. After that trip where we met, I was convinced I'd make aliyah the moment I finished my undergrad, but I never went to Israel again, not even for a visit. The most Jewish thing I've done since my grandmother died is eating a bagel at the Yale Chabad house. Whereas you barely knew you *were* Jewish—'

'Come back to Israel,' I urged. 'We'll go to the wall together. You can write to God.'

'Maybe I'll send a note and you can deliver it for me. I'll ask God for a fully-funded post-doc position and a hot research associate. *Your* prayer worked, after all.'

*

After our call ended, I went into the kids' room to comfort Miriam Celia, who always woke up fussy. It had been so easy to lie, back on the tour bus. Nechama's brash question, yelled over three rows: 'So what *did* you write to God, anyway?' I'd known even then that Nechama was wrong, though I hadn't the slightest idea how deep and rich the truth would be, like drowning in sunlight so radiant even sunglasses couldn't shield it. I'd calmly called back, 'I asked God to protect the IDF soldiers. Especially the ones who dance.'

The first time I walked backwards from the Western Wall, I was dizzy from the heat, from the praying women, from Susie's tattoo and the realisation that tragedy didn't end just because a person survived it. I'd felt so unsteady; how could I ever learn to dance when I could barely walk? But the wall rose up before me, supporting me, as it had and always would. Step by backwards step, I whispered the Shema, the lyrics of 'Am Yisrael Chai', and the words I'd written in my note, knowing that God would hear and understand:

Please make me feel Jewish. Please give me roots.

Adrian Ross
SCALES

He was the only teacher without a nickname. Somehow, his surname said enough. Scales taught history. That was when he wasn't distracted, flirted with by his two favourites at the front, lured into discussions on unrelated themes or simply begged to entertain us differently.

He wasn't entirely a softie, but he credited us with more maturity than we had, so we pretended to like him more than we did. Scales didn't realise when people were messing with him.

'Oh really?' he said, with heart-melting sincerity. 'Which parts of history do you think are not relevant to teenagers' lives?'

Unlike the rest of the staff, Scales was not dead. He didn't sleep-walk through ancient notes, drift off while we read something out or feast on our blood by spending an entire lesson going over homework. He was of average height, with an aerodynamic nose and shiny, gelled black hair.

He dressed too smartly for a teacher. The girls teased him endlessly about his ties, cufflinks and thick-rimmed black glasses. They asked probing questions about his home life (married, with one son) and steered discussions in the direction of sex. He never realised when chats had gone too far, which made them all the funnier.

So it came to pass that we unwittingly launched his political career.

Instead of covering our prescribed exam topic, the Vietnam War, we were bemoaning the Green Party's prospects under the woeful first-past-the-post system. Scales made an idealistic speech insisting we could change things because we are the future, blah blah blah. Someone heckled him, saying we needed change *NOW* and he was in a better position than us to deliver it. Other teachers would have dismissed this out of hand, of course, but Scales walked over to his desk and sat on it, dangling his legs – always a good sign.

'Do you really think so?' he asked, hand on chin.

Yes, we said. Of course. You'd be great! You'd make a difference. You'd change the world, Sir.

Two days later, someone pointed out there was a by-election to the council. We offered to run his campaign and the hilarity began to build. We would knock on doors, design posters, deliver leaflets.

Scales admitted he supported green policies but wasn't really a Green Party chap.

'You should be the SNP candidate,' said one of the girls. 'Then you could change things from the inside.'

'I'm not really a nationalist,' he revealed. 'My mum's from Carlisle.'

'Try the Conservatives, then,' suggested the other girl. 'You can really shake up the establishment.'

'Hmm, I don't know,' muttered Scales. 'I'm actually a Labour voter.'

'But you're not a member,' I said, speculatively, and he nodded.

Then suddenly we were discussing history again; the siege of the United States embassy in Saigon.

Two weeks later, we were due to discuss the founding of the National Health Service. But Scales had an announcement. He'd joined the Tories and their candidate was going into hospital for an operation, so he was now on the shortlist to replace her.

We formed a WhatsApp group there and then. Our best artist was enlisted to produce posters while my friend, who mostly wrote jokes, came up with the slogans. By the end of the lesson we had three designs:

Scales has vision! (Illustrated by a pair of thick-rimmed black glasses).

Scales has energy! (Picture of a bottle of Lucozade).

Scales has got your back! (Diagram of a spine, forming an 'S' shape).

People were deputed to photocopy the posters and others to flypost them shamelessly near the local party office.

'Thanks for your support, guys,' said Scales, beaming.

Our crude campaign worked. The grandees wanted a candidate who evidently had some support and was neither dead nor half-dead. Scales fitted the criteria perfectly.

We started to feel uneasy.

'What if he gets elected?' messaged one of the girls. 'We'll have helped the Tories.'

'No going back now,' replied my friend.

Our resident sage, whose father was a lawyer, pointed out there were strict rules to follow when campaigning. The posters were adapted to meet the requirements of the Electoral Commission. The single design now had no words on it, just a pair of thick-rimmed black glasses, an un-named yellow bottle and a spine in the shape of an 'S'.

The enigmatic posters caused a frenzy of speculation on social media and they were enthusiastically retweeted. Many people guessed correctly they referred to Scales.

Next, the girls talked him into installing the music department PA system in his pitiful car, a small runabout with a child seat. He secured the speaker to its roofrack. 'Vote Scales' pennants fluttered from its windows and matching bunting started appearing in shops and front gardens.

After school each day, Scales persuaded his wife to drive him around town, with junior in the back, while he spoke sincerely into the microphone, between snatches of the song *It's A Family Affair* by Womack and Womack (a nice sardonic touch, that, by the girls). Everywhere he went, pupils applauded. Adults wheeled about, wondering: who is this guy?

Most of the class came to the count. There was a delicious moment when we discovered Scales not only had a first name but a ridiculous middle name, too. It was a close three-way contest, but thanks to the ludicrous first-past-the-post system, our man scraped home to become the fifth Tory on the council.

'I've come into politics to make a better world,' he said, to boisterous cheers. 'Tomorrow belongs to the youngsters. We must not rob them today.'

The handful of Conservative activists looked deeply puzzled.

'. . . of their inheritance,' he added hastily, and they applauded.

Our lessons with Scales became enthralling. We raced through the history content so he could report back on his crazy adventure. There was 'no overall control', so opposition members were involved in many civic matters.

The following week Scales delivered the highly amusing news that he was leading a review of the archive service. There was a need, beloved of Tory dogma, to provide an improved service with less money. We cautioned him against cutting opening times and suggested ways of marketing the service.

Scales also phoned the archivist in a neighbouring authority for advice. Within days there was a proposal for both councils to pay into a merged archive service. This would increase opening times and save money, with no compulsory redundancies. The proposal was approved in record time and Scales was rewarded with a place on the education committee.

Worried about the amount of time we were spending discussing his new role, our teacher made us sit a past paper. He was astonished by the results. We were making better progress than his head of department's class. He relaxed.

'Life is full of possibilities,' he told us. 'It's so easy to compromise on our ideals when we should be championing them ruthlessly.'

Party politics became our plaything. When his own group, hungry for more cuts, advocated sacking education support staff, we goaded him into crossing the floor of the chamber. His sensational move gave the SNP a majority and Scales appeared on the TV news, alongside the council leader.

'As a teacher, I will do whatever is necessary to fight for the rights of disabled students,' he declared. The soundbite went viral. Days later, he became Chair of Education.

The next time we met, to discuss the Highland Clearances, Scales was in a dilemma about whether to support an innovative but expensive project linking school and university teaching in engineering.

'Go for it, Sir!' we implored him. 'What have you got to lose?'

He went for it. Over the next few months, kids who would normally drop out of academic work started to get interested in making things. Under the scheme, they came to school part-time, got paid to do an apprenticeship part-time and spent half a day a week at university. A sharp upturn in school performance statistics would follow.

'You have to be prepared to take a risk,' said Scales, in a BBC documentary. 'Otherwise you'll always be stuck with the same issues and outcomes.'

We sat our prelims and the girls came top, followed by the sage, my friend and me. Next came a few students from the other class. Our teacher was so delighted he gave us free study for three whole lessons.

When there was a by-election to the Scottish Parliament in a hopeless seat, the SNP hierarchy asked Scales to stand.

'Is that not a step too far?' he asked us. 'It's a big commitment, if we're just going through the motions.'

In blatant sarcasm that he failed to read, we urged Scales to go all out for the win.

This time there were slickly produced leaflets picturing the man himself with the party leader and with the already weary-looking Mrs Scales, now expecting their second child. Incredibly, the literature carried the wording: 'The candidate with vision, the candidate with energy, the candidate who's got your back'.

The party organised a coach and we headed to the Borders for a Saturday of rampant campaigning. Our overblown enthusiasm built steadily through the day. The girls fed Scales a line for his soapbox speech, which drew a large crowd.

'I want a better deal for the farmers who are doing the right thing by the environment,' he duly said. You could almost see the hairs standing up on the necks of Tory traditionalists. His agent, used to trotting out agreed party policy, looked stunned.

Later, a group of us watched the count on TV at the sage's house, where his parents treated us to a buffet. Scales stood nervously with his minders, while his opponents shared a joke. I noticed something: he dressed perfectly for a politician.

This time, it wasn't even close. We could tell that by the heaps of votes being counted.

'At least we had a good laugh,' said my friend, ruefully.

'It's hard to bang the nationalist drum where people cross the border all the time,' said the sage's dad, sagely.

The candidates shuffled onstage for the declaration. Was that Scales wiping away a tear? Don't take it so hard, pal, I wanted to tell him.

He won by a landslide.

'I want to thank my wife, who delayed submitting her PhD thesis to make this campaign effective,' he said.

One of the girls protested: 'He never mentioned that!'

As we edged towards exam season, Scales handed in his notice. There was now a surreal atmosphere as we – and an MSP – recapped the rise of the herring industry and mass migration to North America. During study leave, my friend posted news of a reshuffle: our teacher was now Minister for Local Government.

The sun came out and we took our Highers. When we returned for the last few weeks of term, Scales dutifully advertised the sixth form.

'But Sir, you're not going to be here!' wailed the other girl.

She had a point. Without Scales to amuse us, school seemed to have run its course. Many of us took up offers of university places.

Half-way through my first year, the sage reported that Scales had been elevated to Cabinet Secretary for the Environment.

'Ha ha – our mad plan is working!' he added.

Scales made provision for reducing carbon emissions, including a scrappage scheme for diesel cars and hundreds more charging points for electric vehicles. He incentivised householders to replace gas-fired boilers with more sustainable kit. He encouraged more businesses to sign up for renewable energy.

At the SNP conference, I got a press badge as a representative of my student newspaper. I crowded into a session in which Scales was announced as Deputy First Minister. Standing next to Dr Scales, he adjusted his rimless eyewear and declared:

'I'd like to thank 5B, an extraordinary class of mine from my teaching days, who pushed me into politics. They convinced me of the need to make a difference in the world. They made me believe in myself. Above all, they took me seriously.'

J. David Simons
THE WHITE PLACE

We were driving north-west on highway 84 out of Santa Fe towards
the Ghost Ranch, the remote desert location for the cottage of the
late painter, Georgia O'Keeffe. The sun was baking the dusty roof
on our Hertz rental, Bonnie in her flowery summer dress had her
bare legs scrunched up against the glove compartment, a couple
of her crystals twinkled on the dash, and a dream-catcher she'd
purchased from a Native American on the Santa Fe Plaza was
wrapped around the rearview mirror. I drummed my fingers
enthusiastically on the steering wheel, thinking life was looking
pretty good for a Jewish boy out of Brooklyn raised on the Talmud
into a world that tended to be seen in black and white. While out
here in New Mexico it was all reds and yellows and pinks in Georgia
O'Keeffe country.

I had to confess to knowing very little about the artist until
Bonnie had suggested this vacation, our first real outing together
since we had hooked up. Bonnie with her Master's degree in art
history worked at MoMA as a curatorial assistant with an emphasis
on American Modernism so was pretty *au fait* with the work of
Madame O'K. Yet it was with a couple of self-help books and a
yoga mat under-arm that she had approached me at the counter
of the independent bookstore I managed in SoHo, and asked:

'Can you recommend a contemporary American writer with an
appreciation for our country's vast landscape – geographical, polit-
ical and cultural?'

'An interesting question,' I had responded, unused to my
customers asking my advice on anything in these Googled-up,
Amazon-algorithm days.

'Yeah, well, I like to go to the source,' she said. She was still
dressed in what I guessed was her yoga gear – black leggings
and a thin tracksuit top, her caramel-blonde hair tied back except
for a few strands matted against her forehead. A rather pleasant

musky mix of sweat and perfume emanated from her slender post-Hatha frame.

'I'm your man then,' I said, immediately regretting that my choice of words from a Leonard Cohen song represented more of a pick-up line than the purely factual statement it was meant to be.

'I hope you are,' she replied with a similar ambiguity.

I assumed she was still referring to her reading research so I considered Franzen, Joyce Carol Oates, Jim Harrison and Denis Johnson but settled on Don DeLillo's *Underworld* and when she slapped the novel down on my counter a couple of weeks later and told me it was 'absolutely brilliant', our relationship was born. Three months on and Bonnie exchanged her zillion Delta air-miles earned from countless flights to visit her sick mother in Arizona for two airline tickets to Albuquerque, a room at a Best Western boasting a king-sized bed bigger than my New York apartment and this very rental vehicle in which we were now coolly ensconced.

A definite sexual chemistry existed between us along with our shared love of vintage gear, the Chelsea galleries, hiking the Appalachian Trail, and the chicken-over-rice with white sauce from the Halal Brothers on West 53rd Street. But it was the looming chasm of our diverse spiritual backgrounds that I feared threatened our future. Me: an ex-Orthodox Jew turned cynical agnostic who believed we knew nothing about anything beyond our own cognisance. And Bonnie: Southern Baptist migrated to Buddhism, Hinduism, Sufism, crystals (hence the dashboard array), angels, shamans, ayahuasca ceremonies, yoga and chakra dancing who believed if we could just align ourselves with the flow of universal energy, everything would be fine.

It was Bonnie's suggestion we stop at the O'Keeffe Welcome Center in Abiquiu, a small town 'Population: 204', a few miles south of the actual Ghost Ranch. There, she beguiled me with her descriptions of the artist's paintings hanging in the white spaces of the visitors' gallery – the wild beauty contained in O'Keeffe's luminescent landscapes, the meticulously observed close-ups of the desert flowers, the bleached animal bones stark against the warmth of the pink skies. I was also surprised to learn from a video presentation that the painter had been an acquaintance of my favourite British writer, D. H. Lawrence, whose ashes were apparently buried at a ranch not far from where I stood.

I asked an earnest woman at reception if there were any hiking trails close to the centre where two car-weary New Yorkers could get an actual feel for the desert. She very kindly told us about The White Place, a dramatic sandstone rock formation off the beaten track, and the subject of many of Georgia's paintings. The area was apparently owned by the Dar al Islam Education Center which had built a mosque and campus nearby, although John Q. Public was still allowed daylight access over at The White Place site.

*

Despite the air-con being cranked up full, Bonnie had her window down, letting her fingers play in the breeze.

'You know,' she said. 'I feel really joyful at this moment.'

'Yeah, it's been fun.'

'More than that, *mi amigo*. I've got this overwhelming sense of one-ness with this stunning landscape.' She used her wind-blown hand to signify the scenery she was describing. 'And a certain synchronicity. Here's me wallowing in Georgia's sacred space and now we discover your guy Lawrence was buried here too. Art and literature. Coming together. Just like you and me. Don't you feel it too? Like we're in tune.'

To be honest, I was too busy looking for the turn-off through a fly-blown windscreen to come up with a suitable response so Bonnie leaned over and ran her fingers over the back of my neck.

'I sometimes wonder about you,' she said.

'What?'

'Whether you possess a soul.'

I had no time to protest the comment as the turn-off loomed up quicker than expected and I had to brake and swerve off the highway into a single-lane tarmac road which soon turned into a heavily rutted track.

'Jesus. Are you sure this is right?'

'I'm just following directions.'

It was like driving along a giant washboard, my head was almost bouncing off the roof to each ridge and rut while Bonnie was busy scampering around the footwell trying to find her crystals. I had definitely moved the vehicle off any surface deemed acceptable to the terms and conditions of our Hertz rental agreement but I felt we were too far into the journey to turn back. After lurching along like this for another couple of miles we found ourselves outside a ranch-style pole entry-way with the sign *Dar al Islam* hanging off the crossbeam. I gratefully turned off the rutted surface onto a stony uphill track, driving up the dust for a further hundred yards to a flattened-out piece of desert dirt marked out as a parking area with some lengths of timber. As I pulled into this patch of earth, I heard a loud, ominous clunk from the rearside of our rental.

'What was that?' Bonnie asked.

'Must have driven over something.'

I feared we had gotten a flat but when I went out to inspect, the situation turned out to be even worse than anticipated – the entire exhaust pipe and manifold had fallen off the chassis and lay on the ground like some kind of metal corpse under our vehicle. Given that automobile mechanics was not high up on my list of life skills, all I could do was utter: 'We're screwed.' Bonnie meanwhile was jogging around the perimeter of our disembowelled car, holding her cellphone to the sky as if it were a totem to the gods, declaring, 'I can't get a signal. I can't get a signal.'

I checked out my phone and it too was showing we were in a no-bar zone. I kicked one of the rear tyres as if somehow that would make a difference. 'I'll walk back to the visitors' centre, see if I can get some help. You can stay here, if you want.'

'Why don't we go for our hike first?'

'Really?'

'Yeah. Really.'

'I don't think a hike should be our main priority right now.'

'But we're here. In this fantastic place.'

'Yeah, with a broken-down vehicle in the middle of nowhere.'

'I get that. But it's still early. We've got water. We've got time.'

Bonnie stood there with her hands on her hips, her sandaled feet firmly apart. Meanwhile I was thinking about the long walk-out in the heat, finding a garage, calling out a mechanic, the insurance deductibles, the rental agreement violations and expensive tow-trucks. 'Sure,' I said. 'Let's do it.'

*

We descended separately from the parking area on a beaten path through white sage and flowering cacti so it was Bonnie up ahead who first caught sight of the magnificent chalky cliffs. We both stopped and stood in awe at the amazing geological formation of columns and spires and obelisks set in striking contrast against the cobalt sky. I had been to Barcelona a few years back and this was like witnessing New Mexico's very own alabaster *Sagrada Familia* basilica rising out of the dirt. I wanted to share my sense of wonder with Bonnie but she had already skipped on towards a flat-topped boulder set within the rare shade of a desert pine. She sat down cross-legged on the rock, her back rigid, her thin dress high on her thighs, and I could see her belly move underneath the fabric as she breathed in the magic of our surroundings. She brought her hands together in a prayer-like clasp in front of her and closed her eyes.

I let her be, wandered into the slot canyons of these fantastical structures as if I were a tiny creature moving in and out of the legs of a herd of giant elephants, pressing my hands against surfaces that had been shaped and smoothed by wind and water across millennia. I stopped and listened. A thick silence blanketed my surroundings. No far-off traffic, no birdsong, no wind whistling through the gullies. I turned my back to the canyon wall and let myself slide down the chalk surface into a crouch, gulped down a swig of warm bottled water. I took out the information sheet I'd picked up at the Welcome Center. A map showed me that the actual mosque and campus established by the Dar al Islam Foundation lay a couple of miles to the west of where I sat. I closed my eyes and let the oppressive airless heat pull me into a drowsiness within the confines of this desert cathedral.

Beyond Islam and disbelief there is only the desert plain. Yes, I could understand how this Levantine landscape would be entirely appropriate for a centre devoted to the teachings of the Prophet Mohammed.

Or how a painter like O'Keeffe might be attracted to such bleached organic structures.

Ever since it loomed up before me like a mirage, I have been drawn to the white bones of this place.

Or how this bright, lucent landscape might have influenced the life and work of David Herbert Lawrence, the son of a miner, raised in dreary England.

Death is coal black and skeleton blanched. Sunlit and sunless.

I heard Bonnie calling me. I folded up the sheet, put it back in my pocket, and moved back out through the crevasse fissure into the sunshine. She had descended from her perch and was already on her walk back to the car but she stopped and lingered until I caught up with her.

'I was getting worried about you,' she said.

'Why?'

'You were away for ages.'

'Really?'

'And look.' She pointed up towards to the parking area. Another vehicle had drawn up beside our own.

*

Leaning against the hood of his beat-up pickup truck stood a dark-haired, deeply tanned Native American gentleman, staring out at the landscape as he drew on a cigarette. He wore sunglasses, a neatly-pressed pair of chinos, a cream short-sleeved shirt that struggled to restrain his biceps, and a bolo tie with an ornate silver and turquoise clasp. He nodded as we approached.

'We could do with a ride out,' I said, indicating our immobilised vehicle.

He dropped his cigarette, squashed the burning stub into the desert floor with the heel of his boot and said: 'Let me have a look.' He sauntered over to our car, shook his head knowingly at the damage, hunkered down onto his haunches for a closer inspection, then slid smoothly under the chassis in all his clean clothes. Bonnie looked at me as if perhaps this was a course of action I should have taken myself. I shrugged off her gaze, although I felt that even in this age of supposed gender equality, my masculinity had been challenged.

After a few minutes of exploration, our Native American friend emerged again, stood up, dusted himself off and said to me: 'Nope.'

'Nope what?'

'One of the brackets is broke.'

'Can anything be done?' Bonnie asked.

'What we need is a length of wire.'

'A length of wire?'

'Yep. Best have a look around.'

We were standing in a scratched-out piece of badlands in the middle of nowhere so I couldn't help myself saying: 'A length of wire. Here?'

'Hey, this is New Mexico,' the man said, lighting up another cigarette, adding to the day's scorching temperature with a flick of his thumb on a Zippo wheel. 'There's always a length of wire lying around somewhere.'

The three of us started hunting around the makeshift parking lot and then out into the scrub and desert area beyond. It was Bonnie who found the length of wire, about six feet long, twisted around an old fencepost that was as dried-up and desiccated as the bones in one of Georgia O'Keeffe's paintings. She brought her discovery to our saviour in triumph.

'Yep,' he said before disappearing again under the rear of our rental while Bonnie and I stared down quietly at the outstretched legs in the dirt.

Back out into the sunshine with task accomplished, the man pushed himself erect and announced: 'Wired you up a cradle.'

'Will it get us back to Albuquerque?' I asked.

'As long as you don't ride that rutted road again. Turn left instead of right at the gate. You'll have tarmac all the way to just south of Abiquiu.'

I fumbled around in my pocket, offered him the few bucks I had.

'Just really lucky I was here,' he drawled, pushing the money away. 'Hardly a soul ever comes up to this place.' He turned around, got into his truck, and Bonnie and I watched on in silence as this mysterious stranger drove off in a cloud of dust and spitting stones. Once he had gone, she turned and looked at me with those blue eyes I always found so difficult to read.

'See,' was all she said.

Taylor Strickland
DUNDEE

for Jane McKie

Patterns of ashlar, slate. The gable-fronts
gather round in hard shadows and one by one
parked cars, the streets. All are gathered up.

Soft chevrons of white and ashen snow
soundproof this city. I collapse, a drunk
bundled in night, my buttonless greatcoat.

Michele Waering
GAUZE STREET HAVERS

stop go
crisp packets skirl the war memorial,
insinuate health warnings—

red and green pedestrians face redundancy—

rolling rattling
a recalcitrant umbrella refuses to wait
skites past defiant—

gusts thump stained-glass apostles,
moonlight ghosts the abbey close—

threadbare river, dun-coloured fishes:
dizzy-diving moon hits the lights—

walk don't walk

get home—
before kids in too-thin jackets gallivant the streets
jostle for moonbeams
buttonhole red and green pedestrians

Christie Williamson
RETURN

for Gerry

in Victoria Park they've taken
the tennis nets away
but the boy still plays
his backhand pass, making

the da da's outstretched strings
ping at the far reaches
of the white lined tarmac, teaching
each, one and all the thing

to keep your eye on
is the bounce of the ball
the height of your chances

and with the rain dry on
your soles whatever falls
rises again to call the dance

DOMINION

i.m. Charles Nowosielski

liberaetit boadies braithin free
ay shaa dimsels fur whit dey ir
an at da hill's fit trow smirr
an hungry jaas dey wir eence a we

wha'd traded chains fur reins
wha's stage eclipsed page
eftir page fae da golden ages
o growin trow joy an pain

wi da sun saftly touchin doon
ahint da faur side o da loch
a licht persists in dancin roond

da croon o da bairn wha's awppin haund
howlds laek a brokken blackbird's wings
aa da magic o da laund

LOWIN

dir a fire
ahint mi een
nae freen
o da choir

mi feet laund
i da hoofprints
o lost mitts
fur dirty haunds

da air is clear
ayont da windoo
da rod unbrokken

athin me fear
is runnin fu
an isna spokken

Les Wood
STATEMENT

The Playstation was fucked tae begin wi. Somehin tae dae wi the hard drive, or a connection – Ah don't know enough aboot that kinda stuff. Whitever, it wisnae workin. So, the thing wis, me an Deano didnae huv anything tae dae. Daytime telly wis shite, jist Hames Unner the Hammer guff, an, even though we shared some hash (mibbe Ah shouldnae say that, but we did), we were baith bored aff oor tits. Deano wanted tae watch some porn oan the laptop, but Ah wisnae intae that – felt weird tae squish up beside each other oan the setee tae see the screen, luk at aw that shagging an stuff. It wid be too close. Too, whit's the word . . . intimate. So we didnae watch any, but Deano began tae get a bit ratty aboot it. He dis that sometimes, flies aff the haunle when he disnae get his wey. Ah'm used tae it but, so Ah jist let it wash ower me. The hash wis wearin aff though, an we'd nae mair left, so his mood wisnae getting any better. That's when wee Roxy walked in. She'd been sleepin through in the bedroom or the hall, or somewhere, an she mibbe needed to go oot tae the gairden, attend tae her business, dae a jobby or a pee. She nudged Deano's leg an he booted her away. No too hard, or anythin, but hard enough fur a wee thing like Roxy Ah suppose. The dug gave a yelp, an Deano started laughin. Ah laughed a wee bit tae, but mair jist tae humour him than anythin else. Deano lit up a fag, didnae offer me a drag. That wis fine, by the way, Ah didnae care. Then he leaned ower an touched the end ae the cigarette tae the dug's bum. The dug jumped up, yippin, spinnin roon tae see whit had happened. Deano wis laughin harder noo, enjoyin hissel. Ah like that wee dug. It's nice. Friendly. Ah telt him tae lea the dug alane, it wisnae daein us any herm. Deano luks ower at me wi a scowl oan his face, but still kinda laughin, an tells me tae fuck off. Then, he grabs the dug by the collar and drags her ower taewards him. The dug's legs start scrabblin against the flair, tryin tae pull away. Deano yanks it harder an he grips the dug tight. He pit his fag oan the dug's nose, an noo she really howled, struggling tae get away, eyes wide an barin her teeth. Roxy turned her heid an luked up at me. That's when Ah got up an went intae the kitchen. Ah came back oot wi a fryin pan.

Ah didnae stoap.

BIOGRAPHIES

Tha **Seonaidh Adams** na thidsear agus na athair do dà bhalach aig a bheil Gàidhlig, Gearmailtis is an cànan eile. Tha e air a bheòghlacadh le uisge-beatha agus an DDR.
Seonaidh Adams is a teacher and father to two trilingual boys. He is a keen student of whisky and the DDR.

Lorcán Black is an Irish poet. His poetry has been published in *Poet Lore, Stirring, Snapdragon, Connecticut River Review* and *The Los Angeles Review*, among numerous others. He is a Pushcart Prize and Best of the Net nominee. His first collection, *Rituals,* was published by April Gloaming Publishing in 2019.

Sheila Black is the author most recently of a chapbook *All the Sleep in the World* (Alabrava Press, 2021). Her fifth full-length book, *Vivisection,* is forthcoming from Salmon Poetry. Her poems have appeared in *The Spectacle, Poetry,* the *New York Times,* and elsewhere. She lives in San Antonio, Texas.

Kate Coffey was inspired to write 'The Sìth' after researching her Highlands family history. She has previously been published in *Mslexia* and was shortlisted for the Bath Short Story Award 2020. She has just completed a collection of stories, that weave ancient myth and folklore into the modern day.

Oliver Emanuel is an award-winning writer based in central Scotland. He has written over thirty plays for both stage and radio, and is Reader of Creative Writing at the University of St Andrews.

Originally from Alberta, Canada, **Patrick James Errington** is a Scotland-based poet, translator, editor, and academic. Recipient of the Scottish Book Trust's Callan Gordon Award and numerous other prizes, Patrick's poems feature in journals and anthologies worldwide as well as in two recent pamphlets, *Glean* (2018) and *Field Studies* (2019).

Jane Flett is a Scottish writer based in Berlin. Her writing has been commissioned for BBC Radio 4, anthologised in Best British Poetry, Highly Commended in the Bridport Prize, and awarded the New Orleans Writing Residency. In 2020, Jane was a recipient of the 2020 Berlin Senat Award for non-German literature.

Ewan Forbes lives and writes in Glasgow, Scotland. His fiction has previously appeared in *Gutter: The Magazine of New Scottish Writing*, and in *Daily Science Fiction*, amongst other places, and he has had his poetry published in *Popshot Magazine*. He said to say hello, and to wish you well.

Helena Fornells is a Catalan poet based in Edinburgh, where she works as a bookseller. Her poems have appeared in *Harana Poetry*, *Finished Creatures*, *The Interpreter's House*, *DATABLEED*, and the anthology *The Evergreen: A New Season in the North*.

Sally Gales is an ex-architect turned writer. Originally from South Florida, she moved along America's northeast coast, before relocating to Scotland. She obtained a Doctorate of Fine Arts in Creative Writing from the University of Glasgow and now uses her degree to teach. In addition to speculative fiction, Sally writes non-fiction essays around her explorations of Dead Spaces – ruins that are forgotten and thus unseen – and when she's not reading or writing, you can find her hiking, climbing, or baking.

Niamh Griffin is a graduate of the M.Phil Programme in Creative Writing from Trinity College Dublin. She previously worked as a staff writer for *Chat* and *Pick Me Up!* magazines. Niamh lives in Edinburgh with her partner Eva where she now works for the Consulate General of Ireland. They are expecting their first baby this summer.

Joseph Hardy, of Nashville, Tennessee, grandson of William Hardy, (born in Glasgow in 1880), has been published in: *Appalachian Review*, *Cold Mountain Review*, *Inlandia*, *Poet Lore*, and *Structo*. He is the author of a book of poetry, *The Only Light Coming In*.

A. M. Havinden is a writer and artist based in Argyll. In 2020, she was awarded a fellowship from the Scottish Book Trust to develop a collection of poems exploring the waters of the west coast. Her poems, often exploring women's history, have won several awards and been widely published.

Originally from Edinburgh, **Antonia Kearton** now lives with her family in the Scottish Highlands, where she is training to become a person-centred counsellor. She recently started writing poetry again after a gap of over two decades, and has been published in *Northwords Now*, *Still Point Arts Quarterly*, and *Acumen*.

Zachary Kluckman, the National Poetry Awards 2014 Slam Artist of the Year, is a Scholastic Art & Writing Awards Gold Medal Poetry Teacher and a founding organiser of the 100 Thousand Poets for Change programme. Kluckman, who tours as a spoken word artist, was recently one of three American poets invited to the Kistrech International Poetry Festival in Kenya. He has served as Spoken Word Editor for the *Pedestal* magazine and has authored two poetry collections.

Joshua Lander did a PhD on Philip Roth in 2019 at the University of Glasgow and very much regrets his choice of author. He has been published in *Philip Roth Studies*, *Gutter*, and has a chapter in the forthcoming book, *The Holocaust Across Borders: Trauma, Atrocity, and Representation in Literature and Culture.*

Originally from Edinburgh, **Juliet Lovering** lives in Doha where she works as an academic writing instructor and leads the Creative Writing Circle at Qatar National Library. She has published academic articles, popular criticism and prize-winning fiction. For more information, visit **www.julietlovering.com**.

Crìsdean MacIlleBhàin / Christopher Whyte is a poet, a novelist, and a translator. His sixth collection, *Ceum air cheum / Step By Step*, with translations by Niall O'Gallagher, was nominated for two national prizes in 2019. CLÀR published his seventh, Gaelic-only collection, *Leanabachd a' cho-ghleusaiche* (Childhood of the Composer) in 2020. A fifth book of translations from the Russian of Marina Tsvetaeva, *Youthful Verses*, also appeared last year, with Shearsman Books. **www.christopherwhyte.com**.

D. B. MacInnes lives on the Isle of Skye, on the croft his forebears came to in 1860, where he grows vegetables, plays uilleann pipes and writes. He has been published in various magazines including *Gutter* and *Northwords Now* and was longlisted for the Fish Short Story competition in 2019.

Rob McInroy is the author of *Cuddies Strip* (Ringwood Publishing). It was longlisted for the 2021 CWA First Blood Dagger award and was a winner of Bradford Literature Festival's Northern Noir competition. He comes from Crieff and his writing is set in Perthshire, from the 1920s to the present day.

Carol McKay taught creative writing through the Open University from 2004 till 2018. She was awarded the Robert Louis Stevenson Fellowship in 2010 and was shortlisted for the Dinesh Allirajah Prize for Short Fiction in 2019. Her poetry pamphlet *Reading the Landscape* is forthcoming from Hedgehog Press.

Originally from Glasgow, **Mark McLaughlin** lives in East London with his wife and two sons. His work has been listed for the VS Pritchett, Spread the Word Life Writing, and Retreat West prizes and appeared in the *24 Stories of Hope* anthology. Mark is currently working on his first novel.

Robbie MacLeòid is a poet and songwriter who writes in Scottish Gaelic and English. His work has appeared in *Gutter*, *404 Ink*, and *STEALL*. He was StAnza's poet-in-residence in 2020. Robbie researches and teaches at the University of Glasgow.

After retirement, **Thomas Malloch** thought he might try his hand at writing, some of which has even made it to publication. Examples of such work can be found in the *barcelona review*, *Adhoc Flash Fiction*, *Bath Flash Fiction*, *Reflex Fiction* and *Gutter*.

A poet, playwright, and lecturer, **Wendy Miller** lives in the south side of Glasgow with her partner Gillian and their son, Edwyn. Wendy recently graduated with a Masters in Playwriting (with distinction) from the University of Edinburgh. Her 2018 poetry collection *I Am Fire* is available to buy from Category Is in Govanhill.

Marion F. Morrison (Marion F. Nic IlleMhoire) was born on Barra and brought up in Glasgow. She gained the degree of MA and also an MLitt. from the University of Glasgow and was a teacher in Glasgow, and the Western Isles. In 2017 she won the New Writer's Award from the Scottish Book Trust and published her first anthology of poetry (*Adhbhar ar Sòlais – Cause of Our Joy*) in 2018. She is currently working on a new poetry anthology and writing short stories.

Tom Newlands is currently finishing his first novel, which explores disability, class consciousness and female friendships on a seaside council estate in Fife. Portions of the book have earned him a shortlisting for Penguin WriteNow and a 2021 London Writer's Award for Literary Fiction. He is online **@thomas_newlands**

Catherine Ogston lives near Perth. She was a commended finalist in the 2020 Exeter Novel prize and was longlisted at the Caledonia Novel Award 2020 and *Mslexia* YA contest. She has had work included in anthologies by Storgy, Bath Flash, National Flash Fiction Day, Reflex Press and *New Writing Scotland* 35. She was shortlisted for a 2021 New Writers Award at the Scottish Book Trust.

Lauren Pope's poetry has appeared in various publications including *Gutter, Magma, The North, Poetry Wales* and *The Rialto*. She is a 2019 Manchester Poetry Prize finalist. Her first full-length collection, *Always Erase*, is forthcoming from Blue Diode Press in 2022.

Allan Radcliffe's short stories have been published widely and broadcast on BBC Radio 4, and he is a recipient of a Scottish Book Trust New Writer's Award. He has worked as an arts journalist and critic for nearly twenty years.

Tracey S. Rosenberg is the author of a historical novel and four poetry collections. She's Writer in Residence at the University of Edinburgh. 'The Western Wall' was written in situ in Jerusalem, thanks to an Endless Different Ways grant from Creative Scotland as part of the Muriel Spark centenary commemorations.

Adrian Ross worked as a staff journalist in London and South Wales before taking up management roles in the arts and education. Back home in Scotland, he now writes full-time. A novelist and contributor to *Writers' Forum* magazine, three of his plays have been publicly performed, one acted by himself.

J. David Simons is a Scottish novelist whose works include *The Credit Draper* (shortlisted for the McKitterick Prize), *An Exquisite Sense of What is Beautiful*, *A Woman of Integrity* and most recently *The Responsibility of Love*. He is also a previous recipient of the Robert Louis Stevenson Fellowship.

Taylor Strickland is a poet and translator from the US. Currently a doctoral candidate in literary translation at the University of Glasgow, he lives in Glasgow with his wife, Lauren.

Michele Waering's work has appeared in *A Thousand Cranes: Scottish Poets for Japan*; *From Quill to Quark*; *Envoi*; *The Interpreter's House*; *World Haiku Review*; *Red River Review*; *San Pedro River Review*; *The Ghazal Page*; *From Glasgow to Saturn*; *Allegro*; *Rat's Ass Review* and *Panoply*. She lives in Renfrewshire.

Christie Williamson lives in Glasgow where he is co-chair of the Scottish Writers' Centre. His debut pamphlet, *Arc o Möns*, was joint winner of the Calum MacDonald Memorial Award in 2010. His latest full-length collection is *Doors tae Naewye* (Luath, 2020). He comes fae Yell.

Les Wood lives in Barrhead. He has had several stories and poems published in various anthologies. His novel *Dark Side of the Moon* was published by Freight in 2016 and his second novel, *Close to the Edge*, is currently wandering the wilds looking for a new publisher.